ENDYMION AND THE FAE

A tale of Liamec

J. Steven Lamperti

ISBN-13 : 979-8986150185

Lamprey Publishing
LampreyPublishing@gmail.com

Cover titles and frame by James, GoOnWrite.com

The Tales of Liamec

The Wolf's Tooth
By the Sea
Twilight's Fall
The Channeler Trilogy
The Pirates of Meara
Sunshine over Hero
Endymion and the Fae

The Channeler Trilogy

Moon & Shadow
Sun & Dream
Death & Dragon

*Dedicated   to John,
your passing leaves a hole in
the world and in my
heart*

AUTHOR'S NOTE

The name *Endymion*—pronounced en-DIM-ee-un—comes to us from Greek myth—a shepherd boy so beautiful the moon fell in love with him. In some versions, he sleeps forever; in others, he chooses a life of dreams.

John Keats drew on the same myth in his poem Endymion, which opens with the line, "A thing of beauty is a joy forever."

I first encountered the name, though, in Helen Hope Mirrlees' Lud-in-the-Mist, where the character Endymion Leer—and the strange allure of fairy fruit—left a lasting mark on my imagination.

This story is not a retelling of the myth, the poem, or the novel. But if you listen closely, you may hear their echoes in the hills and meadows of Liamec.

ENDYMION

Endymion's life, up to this point, hadn't been very exciting. He was a shepherd's son, and the son of a shepherd's son before that. He had spent a lot of his time watching and counting sheep, which, as everyone knows, is a formula for falling asleep.

So, let's begin with the most dangerous moment in his life so far—a small thrill, to ready us for the adventures to come.

It started with the bleating of a sheep. Endymion was seated at the top of his favorite perch, a rocky prominence high above one end of the mountain meadow, with the flock grazing below. He was practicing playing his flute, which he immediately lowered at the nervous sound from the sheep.

He looked down. Calliope, the lead ewe—named for the muse of epic poetry, of course—and several of her flockmates were staring fixedly, nervously, at something outside the meadow. Something that was hidden from his view by the scraggly trees bordering the edge of the small mountain dell.

If it had been just one sheep, Endymion might have gone back to his flute, but the uneasy stance of a fair number of the flock meant that something was happening. He clambered down from his perch, grabbed his sheepskin pouch—his pocket—from behind the rocks, and took out his sling and small pouch of stones.

As he rounded the edge of the outcrop, he saw Calliope frozen in place, staring at a wolf—gaunt, ribs sharp beneath its fur. Its unblinking eyes fixed on her hungrily, as if weighing the first strike. Endymion's heart clenched for the panicked ewe.

Endymion loaded a stone into his sling, and began whirling it around his head. The time he'd spent practicing loading, unloading, and slinging the leather strap stood him in good stead. He felt the pull of the sling as the stone began to hum through the air.

He shouted to startle the wolf before it could lunge—and loosed the stone in the same breath, a smooth, practiced motion.

It missed. The stone rattled into the underbrush behind the wolf.

Still, the shot had served part of its purpose. The wolf startled and swung its gaze toward Endymion. The expression in its burning, hungry eyes measured him—food or threat?

Endymion quickly loaded a new stone into the sling, and began whirling it into motion. He had at most a few seconds before the wolf decided that its hunger was stronger than its caution.

He released the second stone, putting every ounce of strength he had into the throw. This time the stone flew true.

It struck the wolf square in the face. The creature yelped—then bolted into the underbrush.

Endymion knew the wolf might come back—and soon.

"Calliope," he said, putting a calming hand on the sheep's back, "we get to go home early today."

After that morning, Endymion never again went to the meadow without his sling. It was the first time he'd truly felt fear in the hills—and, though he didn't know it yet, not the last.

T hat had been a year ago. He hadn't seen a wolf since. Nowadays he liked to get to his meadow early. He enjoyed arriving before the sun burned the morning mist off the green slopes of the little valley. It wasn't really his meadow, but one advantage of getting there early was that if any other shepherd brought his or her sheep this high up into the mountains, they would look for another place to pasture. Sometimes he arrived late, or chose to give the meadowland a rest from the grazing and led his flock elsewhere. Still, whenever he could, he brought his little flock early to his meadow.

Endymion loved his meadow. When he sat at a particular spot, high up on the rock escarpment at the top end of the sloping green field, he could see the foothills of the Etenies Mountains spread out below. Or, if he was early enough, he could see the tops of the tallest foothills rising up through the mist.

Sometimes, if he was even earlier than that, the wall of mist meant nothing could be seen outside the meadow at all. On those days, his family's sheep could just be made out through the fog as pale ivory smudges above the mossy greenness of the sward. That was a little too early, since one of his responsibilities was to ensure that all nine sheep were present.

He didn't count them by number but rather by name. The names went through his head as he spotted each one through the mist. He had named them after the nine muses. When fog obscured their differences, he couldn't identify each one by her own name, so he recited the names of the muses in various orders, depending on his mood. Sometimes by precedence among the gods, sometimes alphabetically, and sometimes by the sheep's pecking order within the flock.

Unfortunately, poor Urania was last by each of these

measures. Because of this Endymion felt sorry for her and sometimes gave her a carrot or a slice of apple as an apology.

Endymion had started calling the sheep by the names of the muses when the family had just been keeping six. His mother had told him he was being too ambitious, while his father had just grunted a dismissal of the idea of naming the sheep at all. But the family's fortunes had been good lately, and they'd finally reached the ambitious goal of keeping nine sheep.

When Endymion first named Calliope, she gazed at him with such gratitude in her gentle, soulful eyes that he felt justified in naming the rest.

Endymion had never much liked his own name. His mother assured him that it was one of the good old names, like Demetrius, Phaedra, or Theodora, not one of these modern common-sounding names, like William, Harry, or plain old John. Marj, the village cunning woman, might have encouraged her to believe this. Sometimes Endymion thought it might be nice to be a John—though there were already several in the village. The villagers distinguished between them by referring to one as John the Thatcher and the other as John the Miller.

In some places to the east, he'd heard, people used their profession as their second name, referring to someone as John Thatcher instead of John the Thatcher. Endymion's mother thought that this was scandalously modern, and she couldn't abide it.

Perched atop the steep slope at the upper end of the meadow, watching his sheep below as they wandered past tufts of thistles and munched on tender grass shoots, Endymion often felt a sense of peace that he found nowhere else.

Counting the same nine sheep over and over got a little old after a while. Endymion varied the ways he numbered them, which helped a little. Still, there were only so many times you could confirm the existence of nine sheep, even if they were named after the muses.

Endymion, though, had a secret. He enjoyed his time alone in the meadow with only the sheep for company. He'd spent much of his sixteen years training to entertain himself well.

Endymion's father had taught him to whittle and even gave him a whittling knife on his thirteenth birthday with a gentle grunt of encouragement. He had used this knife to carve himself a fipple flute, taking a straight length of an elder branch, removing the pithy core, cutting the finger holes, and inserting a plug inside one end to direct his breath across an edge he sharpened.

There was a musician in the village. Endymion had pestered the man until he showed him the secrets of his flute and even gave a few pointers about how one played it. Still, he'd had to do a lot of learning by himself out here in the meadow.

Endymion also had his leather sling. A simple strap of hide with a cradle at the center. He kept a small pouch of round stones in his pocket, but one of the nice things about a sling was that the ammunition was easy to replenish.

After making sure that all the sheep were present and accounted for, Endymion would lay his pocket—the pouch with his midday meal and a few other things in it—at the base of the escarpment at the very top end of the valley. Then, he would climb the rocks with his sling and pouch of stones, his flute, or his knife and a piece of wood. Once on top, he had the vale below him, the fluffy white sheep visible either through the mist, or later in the day against the sunlit sweep of the meadow, with the foothills of the Etenies beyond.

As he sat on the ledge, Endymion would either whittle, whistle, or wield his sling, depending on which he had chosen, until it was time to climb down to break his fast. Often, after the noontide meal, he would switch and spend the afternoon on one of the other activities. Sometimes, of course, he would have to climb down if a sheep wandered away from the meadow or if one started bleating its awareness of some danger he had to investigate.

His mother had told him, in a way that made it seem like she had some knowledge of this, of people who read books and stories for entertainment. Unlike most of the people in his village, Endymion could read (she had taught him), but there weren't any books or anything like that in the village except for perhaps some documents in the town hall or books the village priest kept.

Endymion's mother had taught him his letters and numbers with a stick and scratched lines in the dirt. She had taught him quietly, almost in secret, and Endymion considered reading and writing something slightly shameful. No one else knew how to do it or needed to.

However, she had told him the stories he had no way to read. Her name was Helen. When she told him the tale of Helen of Troy, he stared at her wide-eyed and asked, "Was that you, Mama?" Even now, even when alone, Endymion flushed at the memory—though inwardly, he was still convinced that his mother's face could have been the one that launched a thousand ships.

One particular day, after Endymion had played his flute until the sun stood high in the noonday sky, he climbed down from his rocky perch to break his fast. There was a little trickling stream that ran through the meadow. The stream was part of why Endymion liked this spot—it let him and his sheep quench their thirst. The waterway started its journey through the meadow near the base of his stony vantage point. Endymion knelt to take a drink before picking up his pocket with his midday meal. He preferred drinking above the place where the sheep waded and refreshed themselves.

The sheep bleated their contentment from down the meadow as Endymion took a sip of the sweet, cool water. He tried to tell who was making the sounds from their voices. Sometimes, Calliope and Clio sounded the same.

Endymion had spent the morning practicing the tunes he knew on his familiar flute and trying to figure out how to play a new one. The melodies he knew—and the new one he was trying to master—were songs from the village dance. Most of the villagers got together for a dance in the market square every second Saturday. The musician and a few other villagers who could play instruments would play songs, and those townsfolk who were so inclined would dance. Endymion was trying, by memory and ear, to recall a tune from the last dance.

As always, he admired his pocket for a moment before freeing the slender iron clasp that kept it closed and the contents inside safe. It was made, lovingly, of sheepskin, with fleecy trimmed wool still covering it. His mother had given it to him on his last birthday, replacing the simple linen pocket he had before that. When he wore it, with its leather belt, it hung at the center of his kilt, not to either side. Endymion thought it made him look very adult.

He opened his pocket and revealed its familiar contents. He set aside his whittling knife and his current wooden piece, laid his flute on the grass next to them, and put his sling in its usual honored place. Finally, he pulled his food wrap out of the pouch. His mother had prepared his midday meal for him the evening before. It was a simple wedge of cheese and a piece of flatbread. Still, the cheese was made from the milk of the family's own sheep, and the flatbread was baked over the fireplace in their cottage. The taste might always be the same— but it was the taste of home.

His mother wrapped his midday taste of home in a wool wrap to keep the food from shifting around in his pocket. He found a place to sit on a smooth rock.

The meadow was green and lush as Endymion began to unwrap the bundle. The noonday sun cast a gentle, warm glow over the field, though the escarpment partly shaded his spot by the stream.

A surprise waited for Endymion beneath the last wool fold of his wrap.

Somehow, Endymion's mother had found something different for his fast break today. Both the bread and the cheese were not the familiar fare he'd eaten at midday for the last several years. The bread was a golden brown, lighter and airier than the usual flatbread. It was warm and had given an earthy aroma to the rough wool of his meal wrap. The cheese was a delicate yellow, with streaks of blue running through it, and didn't look anything like his family's sheep cheese. There was also a small purple fruit of a kind he'd never seen before inside the bundle.

Endymion lifted the little purple fruit and held it to his nose. He took a cautious sniff. He'd never seen anything like it —neither growing on the mountain nor in the village market. It smelled enticing and delicious. He took a little nibble with his front teeth, cautious lest there was a pit in the middle. It tasted as good as it smelled, and he popped the whole thing in his mouth. It crunched satisfyingly. It was the best thing he had ever eaten. At least, until he broke off a bit of the cheese and bread and bit into them.

Briefly, Endymion just sat, looking at the food before him. He was a bit stupefied, and if one were to be honest, the expression on his face—if anyone had seen it—would have made that evident.

At the edge of his hearing, Endymion thought he heard a sound. It was an odd lilting sound, almost like a person laughing. He lifted his gaze, but there was nothing there except the bushes and trees lining his quiet green clearing and Calliope, Clio, Urania, and the rest munching contentedly on the grassy slopes below.

Endymion fell to his unexpected meal, forgetting the odd

sound entirely in the pleasure of these strange and exotic tastes. Each bite of bread and cheese tasted better than the one before.

After he put the last bit into his mouth, Endymion licked the crumbs and the final traces of purple juice that enticingly stained his fingers off, treasuring each morsel. He'd never tasted anything this delicious in his life. Each nibble was a lifeline thrown to a drowning man. He felt like a new world had been opened up to him.

Woolfold in the Dell was a small village nestled in a crease in the ridges where the Etenies Mountains softened into gentler slopes as they descended into the foothills. There was one road coming into town from the east and a number of little mountain paths that left steeply to the west and slightly less steeply to the north and south.

Endymion led his flock of nine sheep down one of those steep trails from the west. Or perhaps led isn't the right word; Calliope, as usual, led the flock. Endymion brought up the rear, making sure to prod Urania if she seemed to be wandering or spending too much time contemplating her sorry place in the order of things. If she lagged behind too much, he could either pull a piece of carrot from a stash he kept in his pocket or grab her with the hook of his shepherd's crook. When Urania got the carrot instead of the stick, Thalia would sometimes give him a look as if to say, "Why are you rewarding her when I'm the one that's faithfully following in the footsteps of the flock?"

The mountainous trail they followed into Woolfold ended where the packed dirt street, ironically named the High Way, began. Among the few differences between the street and the trail were that the High Way was roughly level, and there were cottages here and there on the floor of the dell. Otherwise, the packed dirt of the lane looked much like the well-trodden soil of the mountain trail.

In addition to the buildings on the vale floor, the slopes on all sides were scattered with compact, tidy cottages. Those not near the rough dirt lanes of the valley bottom could be reached by walkways and trails.

To Endymion, Woolfold was a metropolis. There had to be at least two hundred people living in the village. On the nights of the village dances, there were sometimes as many as sixty people in the market square.

With the fading of the day's light, other shepherds were also bringing home their flocks. Endymion hooked Calliope to bring the flock to a halt at the intersection of High Way and Lamb Lane. They waited patiently, bleating in anticipation of their homecoming, as Leland led his flock past.

Endymion examined the sheep in Leland's flock critically. There were more of them, but Endymion felt their fleeces were too long and too matted. Leland, or his family, had sheared their flock too early. By the end of the summer, the sheep would be suffering from the heat.

He almost shook his head but resisted in case Leland noticed. Leland hadn't been doing a good job of keeping the sheep away from brambles and other rough vegetation. Endymion allowed himself a glow of quiet pride. His family's wool was always the purest and most immaculate.

Leland was dressed similarly to Endymion, though Endymion noticed Leland eyeing his finely turned-out pocket with a faint flush of satisfaction.

"Leland," said Endymion with a nod.

"Endymion," replied Leland, touching the tip of his crook to his forehead.

S till flushed with the warmth of the camaraderie from his lively interaction with Leland, Endymion rushed through the croft yard, herding the sheep through the squawking chickens into the sheepfold. Still, he made sure to secure the fold gate and that there was hay in the hay rack. Calliope bleated her acknowledgment as he closed the gate and headed to the cottage.

His family's cottage was on the eastern side of Woolfold in the Dell. The civilized side, Endymion's mother sometimes said. The village elders lived on the east side. Marj, the village's cunning woman, lived on the east side. The village's only connection with the outside world, the road, entered the town from the east. Those living on the village's west side were closer to the mountains and, therefore, the strange beasts and creatures that sometimes wandered down from them.

"It's not just the creatures," Helen said, "It's the people, too, if you can call them that." Her expression darkened. "The Ogres are much too big, and the Wee Folk too small. They don't know how to grow them the right sizes up there."

Endymion had never seen an ogre, or any Wee Folk. He had seen wolves, wild boars, and once, a bear. His only concern with them was keeping the flock far enough away from them so that no one but him saw them.

"I'm home," called out Endymion as he let the cottage's wooden door slam shut behind him. His mother gave him a look from near the hearth, where she was working at the cooking table. He wasn't sure how often she had told him not to let the door slam.

"If it breaks, your father will have to fix it," she said. "And you know how much work he has already with the fence for the winter pasture and tending the field."

"Sorry," said Endymion. His father just grunted from his seat on the other side of the hearth.

While Endymion kept the flock in his high mountain pasture during the late spring and summer, his father cared for the other livestock, the chickens, the family's one cow, Tansy, and managed the family's modest field. His mother, Helen, maintained the house and kept the garden that grew on the far side. She also carded and spun the wool. Her spinning wheel had an honored place in one corner of the cottage.

The smell of fresh rushes filled the air this evening. Helen must have just replaced the floor matting.

Tansy was a sweetheart of a cow. She was older than Endymion. Her milking-producing days were long past. There had been talk about what happens to an older, non-productive animal on a working croft; Endymion would have none of it. He remembered nights when he was younger, after fights with his mother, when he had gone out to Tansy's stall—warm, hay-scented, and just faintly herbal—on the side of the sheepfold and slept nestled up against her gentle side. He expected to lose this argument sooner rather than later, but he meant to argue it to the very end.

Woolfold in the Dell was a sheep-herding village, though some crofters did other work—like the blacksmith, the general goods merchant, and a few farmers. But the majority of the villagers worked at something related to the sheep. The crofts shared the labor and specialized. For example, Endymion's family kept their herd modest and mostly bartered their wool and spun yarn. Of course, in the fall, they bred the sheep, and in the spring, the new lambs were born.

They timed the shearing of the sheep to be just before the spring lambing. This allowed the ewes to focus on caring for the new lambs without the weight and discomfort of a thick fleece. And for the sheep to not be burdened with the fleece during the heat of the summer. Endymion, his mother, and his father all worked together to shear their sheep.

Endymion liked to pretend to himself that the male lambs and older ewes who were bartered off to other crofts were going to become part of their flocks. Still, he knew that some of them would be traded to the Fleshers and would be returning to the croft in the form of the stews and shepherd's pies that graced the family's evening table.

Endymion's naming system, which he maintained carefully, had to be modified a little each year, as some of the sheep were bartered off, and some of the new lambs replaced them. Calliope and Urania had avoided the misfortune of being replaced by a younger lamb for several years. Calliope had been spared, thanks to her value as a lead sheep. Endymion thought of her as his eye on the trail. She unerringly led the flock along the narrow mountain trails to the higher pastures.

Urania had survived through some form of luck. Her thin frame made her look younger than she was, and she had somehow managed to be overlooked during the selection process for the last few years.

Leland's family kept several rams in their flock. They were the ones most of the crofts turned to in the fall for breeding. Endymion sometimes envied Leland the challenge of guiding a flock containing rams.

Lately, Woolfold in the Dell had been enjoying something of a renaissance. Some people in the cities of Liamec had discovered the quality of the textiles from the small Etenies mountain villages. Just last week, a trader from distant Capitol, where good king Twilight lived, had rolled his cart into town. At first, Endymion's father had stared blankly at the coins the man tried to hand him for a bolt of wool, but Helen gazed at the money, did a quick mental calculation, and grabbed it enthusiastically.

The way Endymion's family decorated their home was a little unusual. The wall space that wasn't occupied by wooden shutters held either his father's wood carvings or his mother's embroidery. The carvings were scenes of nature. They showed the animals, mountains, trees, and hills of the land around Woolfold in the Dell—in carefully, lovingly shaped wood.

They were Endymion's father's primary means of expression. One carving, which had always particularly fascinated Endymion, featured a little person—a tiny woman, or so it appeared—peering into the scene from one edge. As a child, he had spent hours studying the tiny figure. Had a Wee Folk woman once watched his father carving?

When Endymion asked his father about this carving, all he got in reply was an expressive grunt. His father had many grunts, each with its own meaning. This one was unique—and one Endymion had never heard in any other context.

The embroidery that decorated the remainder of the walls was filled with Endymion's mother's wisdom. Unlike some embroidered sayings, they didn't say things like "*Home Sweet Home*" or "*Bless this House.*" Instead, his mother's lore ran more to things like "*Danced with Kings, now counting sheep,*" "*Keep your friends close, and your sheep closer,*" "*Sheep happen,*" and "*Never bring a knife to a sword fight.*"

That last saying rang true to Endymion, though he had never seen either his mother or his father with a weapon more lethal than a shepherd's crook.

More serious than the messages on the embroidery was his mother's locked trunk in one corner of the loft. Endymion had never seen it open. It was an elegant thing, with inlaid wood arranged in glorious patterns. Since his bed had been moved to the loft, Endymion had spent many a night admiring its beauty by candlelight—just as he had with his father's carvings. There weren't any pictures in the patterns, but he had often felt that if he stared long enough, he might start seeing something hidden.

When he was younger, he had asked his mother what was in the trunk. She said, "The past," and then added, "It's best left alone." Soon after, a new embroidery had appeared on one of the last bare patches of wall: *"Old wool makes for tangled threads."*

Endymion knew where the key to the trunk was. There weren't many places to hide things in their cottage. His mother had a small jewelry box that she kept by her bed. And though curiosity nibbled at his mind like a sheep at a tender clover shoot, he'd never seriously thought of opening the box—let alone the trunk.

As they sat around the cottage's finely crafted dining table, another example of Endymion's father's woodworking skill, Endymion looked at his mother. She was elegantly dressed, especially for a little village like Woolfold. Her woolen overdress, worn over a linen shift, was of her own making. The design she had worked into the dress reminded Endymion of the patterns in the wooden inlay of the trunk in the loft, though, once again, no specific symbols or images stood out in the weave. His father, sitting on the opposite side of the table, was more simply clad in a plain beige wool tunic over a linen shirt and woolen breeches.

"Mother," said Endymion formally, "I want to thank you for my midday meal today." He smiled at her, his memory of the food's flavors making his gratitude very genuine.

Helen looked a little surprised. "Of course, dear," she said as she scooped a portion of the evening meal, a shepherd's stew, into his bowl, "You need something to eat when you're working up there so high on the mountain."

"I don't know where you got it," said Endymion, "But the bread and cheese were amazing. And," he hesitated, "what kind of fruit was that?"

Endymion's father looked up from his bowl, gazed at his son, and grunted.

Helen's ladle paused mid-scoop. "Fruit?" she repeated, too lightly. "What did it look like?"

Endymion nodded. "Purple. It was delicious."

Helen wiped her hands on her apron, though they were already clean. "Endymion Silas Poimen," she said, "Let's not do this tonight." Her frown deepened, and she gestured toward Endymion's father across the table. "You can see how it upsets your father."

Endymion's father looked up from his stew again, a small bead of broth dropping off one end of his ample mustache, and grunted inquiringly. Not his usual grunt. A different one—harder to place.

Helen continued, "I packed what I pack every day." She shook her head. "The bread was the flatbread I cooked last night over the hearth, and the cheese came from our own sheep." She waved a hand at the shuttered windows on the side of the house toward the sheepfold. One of the sheep bleated loudly at that moment as if to prove her point; the sound made its way, as did a bit of the chill night air, through the wooden slats.

"Dreams are fine in the meadow," said Helen. "But I'll have no more talk of strange fruit at the dinner table." She tousled Endymion's hair, a little more roughly than was comfortable, and looked again at her husband, who had returned to his stew.

Marj, the village cunning woman, felt it was part of her duties to visit various folks in town. Today she was sitting at Helen's table, drinking a cup of chamomile tea. The steaming cups had just been poured. Marj waved a hand over her cup to waft the vapors toward her nose.

Marj claimed she was named after the spice marjoram. "Good for what ails you," she said. She came from a long line of village cunning women. She had learned her cunning from her mother, who had learned it from hers. There didn't seem to be any men involved, and the children of the village sometimes wondered exactly how this worked. Or at least they did after their peers informed them about the birds and the bees and what the more important differences were between boys and girls.

Marj was a big woman. Some of the not-so-nice children in the village referred to her as "Large Marge." However, they were careful not to do this where she could hear them, as there was a local legend about a boy Marj had overheard being cruel, who had supposedly spent the rest of his life with large blue spots on his face.

Helen had never seen anyone with blue spots on his face, so she doubted the truth of this rumor.

"I've always told you there was something special about Endymion," said Marj. "You know, the only child of a seventh son of a seventh son."

Helen shook her head. "Ewan doesn't talk to any of his siblings much anymore," she said. "And besides, some of those sons were actually daughters."

"Seven is seven," said Marj. "And a daughter is at least as good as a son, if not better."

Helen set down her cup, untasted. "But the fruit?" she

asked.

Marj looked up. "Helen," she said calmly, "I didn't think you were the type to go chasing old stories."

She took a slow sip of her tea. "The Wee Folk live in these hills, just like we do. They grow their own food, and some of it's unfamiliar. But it's not magic. Just different."

Helen didn't blink. "And the Red Spring?"

Marj blanched.

"That was before you moved to Woolfold," she said grimly. "You wouldn't know about it."

She hesitated, then drew a steadying breath.

"It won't happen again," she said. "Not this time."

A nother reason why Endymion wished for the simplicity of a name like John—even John Shepherd, which was what he might well have been called if the other villagers had named him after his profession—was the indignity of having three names. Before he'd been old enough to lead the sheep to the high pastures, he'd had several years of relative freedom to run around town with his peers—Leland among them. He'd spoken to them about his and their names. None had more than two names. A few had two; several had just one, but no one but himself had the full, heavy quota of three.

As he lay on his straw pallet in the loft that evening, Endymion pondered this injustice, as well as the other, more recent one, of not being believed about his midday meal. His mother had refused to talk anymore about his bread and cheese and certainly not about the fruit, telling him, again, to stop imagining things.

Endymion thought, somewhat resentfully, that the main reason why he imagined things was because of the stories and fairy tales she had told him when he was younger. Though he had to acknowledge that he had made things up sometimes. The story of the boy who cried wolf came unbidden to mind, and he was embarrassed to feel how well it fit.

If his mother didn't know anything about it, thought Endymion, where had the fruit, bread, and cheese come from? The idea that it might really have been imagined crossed his mind. The idea crossed his mind like a sheep looking for its vanished flock—turned its head from side to side, bleated once, and then wandered off to places unknown. Endymion was sure that he hadn't imagined his midday meal. He licked his lips, and for a moment, he felt he could still taste the heavenly flavor of the fruit.

If he hadn't imagined the delicious meal, where had it come from? His mother had handed him the wrapped parcel in the morning, and it had been in his pocket until he'd taken it out to eat. Endymion hesitated, an unsettling feeling of disquiet filling him. His pocket had been lying at the base of the rock outcrop he climbed each day to watch over the sheep. Could someone have replaced the contents of the meal wrap?

Easing his way out of his bed, Endymion listened for the sounds of his parents from below the loft to see if they were enfolded in slumber. The subdued rise and fall of his mother's steady breathing and the erratic rumble of his father's snore, sounding a little like a petulant beehive, told him they were asleep.

The moonlight streaming through the smoke hole above the hearth and the glow from the banked fire were just enough for Endymion to see by. He clambered down the loft ladder silently and crept over to his mother's work corner. Peering through the gloom, he found her ribbon box, where she kept the pieces of adornment for special clothing projects. With satisfaction, Endymion took a short length of ribbon in his hand, climbed back up to the loft, stuffed the ribbon into his pocket, and went to sleep.

T he following morning, Endymion's mother handed him his meal wrapped in its familiar cloth as he left the cottage on his way to the sheepfold. He gazed curiously at the tight bundle as if the exterior might hold some clue to this mystery. He unwrapped a corner of the fabric, peeked inside and gave it a sniff. It was the smell and sight of his familiar midday meal. Nothing exotic or unusual. Endymion's stomach growled slightly—he was a hungry young man, after all.

He reached into his pocket with his other hand and pulled out the ribbon from the night before. In the light of day, he could see it was bright red. He reminded himself to return it to his mother's ribbon box, hopefully before she missed it. Carefully, Endymion tied the ribbon around the wool wrap—snugly in a bow. He put the bound wrap back into his pocket.

The sheep were, as usual, eager to get out of the fold and start on their trek to the high pasture. Calliope led the way enthusiastically. Endymion thought sometimes that it might be nice to be as content in life as the sheep in his flock. Each day, they fell to the dewy, leafy grasses of the same meadow as if it was a fresh new five-course meal, and they hadn't eaten in days. Then his mind flashed back to the midday meal he had eaten yesterday, and he lifted one corner of his kilt to wipe the drop of saliva that collected at the edge of his mouth.

Clio looked over at him as he dropped the kilt back down. She bleated her disapproval. Judging by the look she gave him, she'd caught a glimpse of something she didn't care for.

"So sorry, my Lady," said Endymion. "So sorry if my behavior isn't up to the standards that you are used to on Mount Olympus."

Endymion kept a careful eye on his wards as they made

their way through town and then up the narrow winding paths toward the high pastures. For the most part, they followed each other, but every now and then, one would start to wander. Endymion discouraged this with a gentle nudge from his shepherd's crook.

When they got higher, he paused occasionally to look back behind them. There wasn't much to see this morning, as the early fog was still clinging to the mountainside and filling the valleys below. It made the bushes and trees along the sides of the path into mysterious strangers that eased their way out of the mists, swaying greenly beside the trudging sheep.

At the base of the rock outcrop, Endymion set down his pocket before climbing to his daytime perch. He glanced at it, weighing whether to bring it along. His mother had taught him the methods of the Greek and Islamic scholars — how to form a notion, test it, and see it through. An experiment, once begun, must be left to run its course. To prove his hypothesis, the pocket had to stay where it was.

Still, he allowed himself one look inside, checking the ribbon tied around the meal wrap. The sight of the bright red bow steadied him, and he set the pocket down again before starting to climb.

Endymion had thought sometimes that it wasn't a good idea to climb these rocks and be further away from the sheep if something needed tending to. Still, he loved the view from the top, and it allowed him to see the entirety of the little meadow. And, anyway, the flock was content to graze peacefully most of the time. He'd had to climb down now and then, but not often enough to outweigh the pleasure he got from his lofty perch.

Today, he brought his whittling knife and the block of wood representing his latest carved creation. He had considered taking both his carving knife and his flute to the top of the escarpment with him, but he liked to concentrate on one thing at a time. Endymion felt that you got more out of something if you focused on it for a longer time—more value and more pleasure as well.

On days when he brought his sling and a collection of rounded rocks to his high seat, he would practice whirling the sling with a rock in it and releasing it at bushes or other targets he could spy from the heights until he ran out of stones. Those days, he would collect small round rocks from the trail as he led the sheep to the pasture.

He was carving a sheep. He had carved the body's basic shape and was working on giving the animal features that specifically resembled Urania. Endymion felt that Urania deserved some recognition for the difficulties of her life: the disrespect of the other sheep, always being last in line, and even being counted last. Perhaps a statue in her likeness would compensate for some of that.

The problem was that making the carving look like Urania and not just like any sheep was difficult. This wasn't helped by the wood he had chosen. He was using a piece of spruce wood. This made it easy to carve, but the soft-grained wood resisted his attempts to carve the fine details he felt Urania deserved. He wished he had started with a piece of birch, or maybe rowan wood.

With his whittling knife in one hand and the unfinished carving in the other, Endymion began to work.

LILY

There was a flower that grew in certain very secluded places in the mountains of Liamec which the locals called the fire lily. Part of the reason for this name is that the plant's flowers were as brilliantly red as a blazing campfire's heart. Another part is that the plant only bloomed after a wildfire had swept across a slope. For the locals, the red blossoms covering the hillside were an unmistakable sign of the rebirth of nature and the return of life to the blackened mountain.

In addition to the color, the sweet honeyed fragrance of the flowers drifted down the slopes, enveloping any passersby in the vibrant scent of new life.

Now, a modern flower expert might tell you that plants like this are native to South Africa and would never have been found in Liamec, which was, after all, somewhere in northwestern continental Europe. To such an expert, there's not much one can say. This is just a humble chronicle of these events and is only what has been recorded of the history, magic, and biology of the land of Liamec. Expertise aside, one can only relay the information one has.

Aside from their value as a source of inspiration to the mountain people after a fire's devastation, the fire lily blossoms were prized for another reason. Once cleared of debris, the collected flowers, when placed in a pot, boiled, and combined with the right ingredients, made a vibrant red dye. This dye was the brightest form of red known to the locals, and, therefore, after a fire, the blossoms were carefully harvested, dried, and kept.

Endymion's mother made sure to harvest only some of the flowers on a given site. She would carefully gather one flower in ten—or one in five if the hillside was lush with the blooms.

The red tide carpeting the hill was part of nature's regrowth. It needed to be respected, honored, and maintained as such.

The red ribbon that Endymion tied around his food bundle was dyed with pigments made from fire lily petals.

Endymion, as usual, became absorbed in his whittling. The tip of his tongue stuck out of the corner of his mouth, and he hummed a wordless tune as he used the knife to coax Urania's soul from the little piece of spruce. With occasional glances to make sure all the sheep were accounted for and his ears alert for any concerned bleating, the hours melted away.

When the sun had reached a certain familiar spot in the sky, Endymion sighed and, gripping both the finished carving and his knife in one hand, began to climb back down the rock. When he reached the bottom, he looked anxiously at his pocket, checking for any sign it had been disturbed.

There was nothing to be seen from the outside. It appeared to be in the same place he had left it. Endymion put down his knife and carving and picked up the sheepskin wallet. He freed the little metal clasp and peered inside.

It was immediately apparent that it had been opened. The red ribbon Endymion had tied around his food packet in a simple bow had been redone. The ribbon was tied in an intricate knot of looping twists. It looked like something he imagined wouldn't look out of place on a noble's table, ending with the bright red ends of the ribbon trailing like whispers across the coarse wool of the bundle. It was so artfully done that he stared at it for a moment, reluctant to disturb the perfect folds. He almost felt as though untying it would break a spell.

Of course, hunger got the better of him quickly. He felt he could already smell the nectar of the fruit that had been in the previous day's meal. He pulled on the ends of the tied ribbon, and it came undone easily. Bread, cheese, and a fruit like the one he'd eaten the day before tumbled softly from the bundle.

For a moment, Endymion felt a sense of satisfaction at

the success of his scientific experiment. Someone had opened his pocket and replaced the contents. He scanned the clearing's edges to see if anyone was watching him. Then, seeing no one, he took the tender, sweet fruit in his hand and bit into it eagerly.

Endymion fell upon his welcome meal, savoring the half-familiar flavors and textures while ignoring the little voice in the back of his head that said he should be more careful. "Idiot," the little voice said. "This could be poisoned. Or, it could be a trap, and someone is watching you right now, planning how they're going to take your sheep."

Someone with food like this wouldn't want my sheep, Endymion thought in response, popping the last scrap of cheese into his mouth. He remembered the taste of the mutton stew that his mother had served at the dinner table last night. It hadn't been bad, but the bread and cheese from his wrap conjured visions of a table spread with foods that were otherwise beyond his imagination.

He heard a noise and lifted his head. The last little crumb of cheese started to fall from the corner of his mouth. Instinctively, his hand leaped to catch it, and almost without his willing it, it made its way into his mouth.

The sound resolved into a lilting laugh, which wafted clearly through the air like bold dancers from a traveling troupe.

Each peal of laughter twisted and swayed its own way across the breeze of the clearing.

They leapt and spun freely through the stillness.

Endymion knew that sound. It was the sound some of the girls made at the bi-weekly dances in the village square when the older boys talked to them and sometimes when they danced.

He looked at the right-hand slope of the valley. He wasn't at his usual perch atop the escarpment, but he could still see most of the meadow spread out before him. There was a brief rustling in the shrubs. He caught a glimpse of something red.

His pulse quickened. Someone was here, maybe watching

him. The laugh still rang in his ears.

Endymion raced across the sward toward the bushes that had been rustling. The red color he had briefly spotted vanished. He tried to place what the color reminded him of.

Was it the red of the final light of sunset gleaming on the thread on his mother's spindle as it spun the family's wool into yarn?

Was it the red of the fire in his family's hearth as his mother told him stories in the evenings when he was younger?

Was it the red of dawn sun streaming in the open door when he watched his father leave the house in the morning to go work on the croft?

His breath caught. It struck him—it was the red of fire lily blossoms on a slope, as life returned to a burned hillside.

At supper that evening, Endymion asked his mother a question. He felt as though he were reverting to childhood. The evening meal, as he had been growing up, used to mean listening to his mother tell stories about the broader world outside Woolfold, with his father occasionally chiming in with a grunt of approval or disagreement. Recently, they had more often eaten in silence, with the occasional discussion of matters of the croft or village events.

"Mother," said Endymion, "Who lives out that way?" He swept his hand across the cottage wall toward the west.

"I think you mean over there," said his mother with a frown, pointing toward the east wall. "And, you know—we've talked about this before." Her frown changed to an expression of concentration, familiar to Endymion, as that was how she looked when she told a story or relayed other facts.

She continued. "The villages, towns, and cities of the Western Marches surround us, ruled over by our good Baron. Beyond the marches, to the north, lie Ashton, the Academy, and then the sea. Eastward lies the center of Liamec, with its great cities—Capitol, Grisput, and on the coast, Ardstead…"

"Mother," Endymion interrupted, shaking his head. "I didn't mean that way—I meant to the west." He pointed again toward the windowless western wall of the cottage. The weather often swept down from the mountains—cold and wintry, or wet and blustery. Many of the cottages in the village had fewer windows on the west side, toward the weather.

Helen frowned again. "No one," she said, her voice firm but not unkind. "Maybe the occasional hermit."

It was Endymion's turn to frown. "Mother," he said, "You know that's not true." He shook his head. "The Wee Folk? The

Ogres? And besides, someone must live on the other side of the mountains. They can't go on forever."

"Can't they?" Helen asked, her voice quieter now. "The Etenies are so high as to be virtually impassible until you get to the Poignant Pass, far to the southeast, or the coast to the north." Helen's brow knit. "The Ogres are inhuman monsters. And, the Wee Folk?" If possible, her expression got even darker. "We don't speak of the Wee Folk."

T he mist was still cloaking the grass when Endymion got to the clearing the following morning. He paused, considering what to do. First things first, of course. He made sure that the sheep were contentedly munching away on the dew-covered greenery.

But, as for his mysterious scarlet visitor, he didn't feel threatened. The replacement of his meal felt like a friendly act, and whoever it was, they seemed more shy about being seen than he was.

There was a spot near the base of his escarpment where a person might crouch under the overhanging rocks behind a low shrub, nearly invisible. Endymion had often thought of this place as somewhere he could hide if something catastrophic were to happen. The idea of hiding instead of tending the sheep was hard to think about, but there had been known to be bandits in the mountains sometimes; ogres were real, though Endymion had never seen one, and he didn't even know what to think about the Wee Folk. His sling, while it was a useful tool for scaring off the occasional wolf, wouldn't be much use in a real fight.

Endymion had tied the red ribbon around his meal wrap again. He carefully placed his pocket in its usual spot, removing his flute, as if preparing to climb the escarpment like always. His plan would only work if whoever had replaced his food wasn't already here watching. Still, he needed to make things look normal. He scanned the bushes around the upper end of the meadow for any telltale glimpse of red before secreting himself in his hiding place.

The view was restricted. Endymion couldn't see the sheep very well at all. For a moment, he had a pang of doubt. Was he endangering the sheep, his family's livelihood, for this? He shook his head. The sheep were well used to this glen, and he shouldn't have to wait here long, just long enough to catch a glimpse of his quarry. The one place he could see, quite clearly, was the spot on the ground where he had left his pocket.

Time crept by. Endymion had brought his flute with him, not his whittling tools, and he was reluctant to play for fear whoever he was waiting for would detect that the sound was coming from the wrong place. He had nothing to do but watch.

Endymion had gotten good at watching. As a shepherd, that was a lot of what he did every day. That said, his flute playing, whittling, and practicing with his sling helped him pass the time. Today, there was nothing but the anticipation to hold his attention. It was enough, however. His heartbeat raced like the village windmill's sails when a storm came through. There was a difference between watching the sheep and watching for a mysterious stranger.

After he had been waiting for what felt like a lifetime, a young woman stepped, as silent as a secret, into his line of sight.

The first thing Endymion saw was the hair. It was impossible to overlook. The young woman's long hair was gathered into several loose plaits that trailed down her back. Her hair color was a red so vivid, it hardly seemed real. It reminded Endymion of nothing so much as the color of the fire lily flower. A memory stirred—gathering blossoms with his mother on the slopes after a fire.

Then he noticed her lips. They were almost the same color. He got lost, for just a second, in the lushness. He'd never seen lips that color before. If you'd asked him, he'd have said that lips couldn't be that red.

She was dressed in a linen tunic, belted at the waist. The tunic was embroidered in patterns and colors that were new to Endymion's eyes. The deep blue of woad, the earthy yellow of a marigold dye, and, of course, the red of the fire lily. The patterns reminded him of those on his mother's trunk, but the similarity faded, and they began to look strange and exotic. Her cloak, worn over the tunic, was open in the front. Its color almost matched the green of the vegetation behind her. If she had the hood up and the cloak drawn around her, she would have been elusive to the eye.

She was breathtaking—unlike anyone Endymion had ever seen before. Her eyes turned up at the corners as if she were sharing a mischievous secret with him. Her features were so perfectly formed that he felt he would stare at them all day, given the chance.

Like a roe deer, she moved gracefully yet hesitantly. Endymion tensed in silence so as not to shatter the moment. Her eyes were fixed on his pocket as she approached it with quiet intent. In her hand was a small bundle, which he guessed must contain the food she intended to put into his meal wrap.

Endymion drew a startled breath. He'd been so focused on her face that he'd failed to recognize one aspect of her appearance. She was petite. If she stood next to him, she might not reach much higher than his waist—though everything about her seemed more mature and graceful than her size would suggest.

Like the roe deer he had compared her to in his mind, she startled at the sound of his in-drawn breath. In one smooth motion, so fluid he barely saw her move, she drew her cloak around herself, turned, and bolted toward the green wall of shrubs at the edge of the glen.

L ater, at the supper table, Endymion steeled himself. His mother was not someone you wanted to cross, but she knew more than anyone in his life, except perhaps for Marj. And, after all, he wasn't breaking any rules—just asking questions.

"Mother," said Endymion, his voice steady, "Why don't we talk about the Wee Folk?"

Helen frowned. Endymion's father, on the far side of the table, grunted.

"We don't," she said. "Because we don't."

Endymion steeled himself further. Fortune favors the bold.

"But why, Mother?" he asked. "Are they dangerous?"

"Eat the fairy's fruit and lose your way," warned Endymion's father, "her sweetness lures—but shun the fae."

Endymion looked at his father in astonishment. It was one of the longest speeches he had ever heard from him.

Helen frowned again. "Your father's too wordy," she said, "but he's not wrong." She glanced at the wooden carving on the wall—the one Endymion had always thought showed a small woman peering in. "They're different from us. They keep to their part of the mountains, and we keep to ours." She looked thoughtful. "Some people think that what's on the other side of the Etenies is Fairyland. They say those who are lured there by the fairy fruit and the Wee Folk's other wiles never return."

Endymion stared at his mother for a moment. "Have you been there?" he asked. "Have you seen it?" He wouldn't have asked if he didn't know she hadn't grown up in Woolfold, and before she had become a shepherd's wife, she had traveled to other places in Liamec.

Endymion's father snorted. This reversion to his nonverbal speech patterns was somehow reassuring to Endymion.

Helen shook her head and gave her son a glance of disbelief. "Of course not," she said. "What did I just say about people who get taken there and never return?"

She looked thoughtful for a moment. "Anyway," she continued. "No one knows where Fairyland is or how the Wee Folk come and go from there." She looked down at the tabletop for a moment. "Or even if they really do."

"But…" said Endymion.

"That's enough about that," said Helen firmly, her tone leaving no room for further discussion. Endymion was grateful to have gotten this much out of her. "Let's talk about something more important—like sheep."

E ndymion wasn't sure how to approach his day. It was no longer a secret he was aware someone had been replacing his meals, so hiding wouldn't help. And tying the red ribbon around his food bundle again seemed unlikely to gain him anything.

As he herded the flock up the narrow mountain trail toward the higher pastures, he considered going to another meadow altogether to avoid the situation. Then, a flash of fire lily red—and the face of the young woman from yesterday— rose unbidden in his mind. He found himself guiding the sheep toward the familiar vale. In fact, it would have been a challenge to steer them elsewhere, as Calliope had a mind of her own, and she loved that meadow as much as he did.

There was no one in the valley when they reached it. The morning mist still clung to the dewy grass, leaving one uncertain where the vapor in the air ended and the dew began. Endymion wasn't sure if he was disappointed or relieved. He'd imagined a wide range of possibilities: from the maiden he'd seen yesterday awaiting him with a smile on her lips, to an army of enraged Little Folk ready to kill him for daring to look at her.

The sheep didn't care. From their perspective, nothing had happened yesterday.

Endymion was struck by a horrible thought. What if he had frightened her away? What if he never got a chance to see those red lips again?

He scanned the edges of the clearing carefully. Remembering the girl's green cloak and how difficult he had imagined it would be to see her if she were enclosed in it, he studied every inch of the bushes and scraggly mountain trees. There was no one there—only him and the sheep.

Endymion sighed and took his flute out of his pocket. He put the wallet in its usual spot and climbed the rocks up to his perch. He wondered if he was lacking in imagination. Still, he couldn't think of anything to do other than to go about his usual routine.

While practicing with his flute and keeping a watch on the sheep below, Endymion kept a careful eye on the undergrowth at the edges of the meadow. He watched for any trace of red among the leaves.

As the sun crept up in the sky towards its midday height, Endymion's feelings clarified. He hadn't been sure whether he was disappointed or relieved. Well, now he knew. Without a doubt, he was disappointed. Something exciting had been about to happen, and now it looked like it had slipped away. And besides, he wanted to see that face again.

When Endymion climbed down from the escarpment and reached the base where he had left his wallet, she was there—waiting for him.

At first, Endymion didn't see her. The mottled green and brown colors woven into her cloak blended with the hues of the meadow and the greenery behind her. When he did see her, he froze, unwilling to move in case she startled away once more. The entire flock of sheep could have run, bleating, out of the meadow, and Endymion wouldn't have moved.

She reminded him again of the roe deer that he had imagined the last time he saw her, though there was a feeling of strength beneath the readiness to flee. Her cloak was closed, making her face the only part of her that he could see outside of the green and brown fabric.

They stood that way for what felt like forever. The only thing that moved was their eyes as they studied each other.

Then, at the same instant, they both moved. Endymion reached carefully to put his flute, still in his hand, down on top of his pocket, and the girl brought out a bundle from underneath her cloak and extended it out toward Endymion.

Each flinched at the sudden movement of the other after the prolonged stillness. Endymion went still again.

Then the young woman started to laugh. It was the same lilting sound Endymion had heard before. It filled him with joy. Her light laugh blended with the murmur of the wind rustling through the leaves of the scattered, mountain-diminished beech trees around the clearing. It formed harmonies with the sing-song voice of the brook's waters. Endymion started to laugh as well.

He finished putting down the flute and looked at the bundle she was holding out towards him. It didn't look too different from his meal wrap, at least not in size and shape. It was a little bigger, and the fabric that was wrapped around the contents was like nothing Endymion had ever seen before. It was vividly colored, with hues brighter than any he was used to, and the weave was tighter than anything that came from his mother's loom. He shook his head—no one in Woolfold would waste such a fine piece of fabric to wrap someone's midday meal.

He took it, hesitating as he both hoped—and hoped not to—touch her fingers, and untied the string bound around the fabric. Inside was the same fare the young woman had given him before: golden, warm bread, blue-veined cheese, and purple fruit. The smell rising from the bundle made his mouth water. He quickly wiped the side of his mouth with his hand, glancing at her to see if she was watching. She was, but she didn't seem bothered by his actions; instead, she was smiling.

Somehow—without Endymion knowing how—and without a word exchanged, they wound up sitting by the side of the brook, both food bundles open between them, breaking their noontime fasts together.

E ndymion was embarrassed at first when his meager food sat beside the contents of the young woman's meal wrap, but she didn't seem to feel the same way. She reached for the flatbread that his mother had prepared the night before. Encouraged, he picked up the piece of fruit from her packet and took a bite.

Endymion stole glances at his meal companion as they ate—trying not to stare at first, but more openly when she didn't seem to mind. The beauty he had seen the day before was even clearer now that they were sitting so close. Her skin was smooth, flawless. Endymion wondered what it might feel like to touch it.

Her eyes were a striking green. The color made Endymion think of the depths of a forest, with majestic trees towering overhead—the kind of trees that didn't grow on his mountainsides, except in a few protected groves where streams had carved valleys into the rough rock.

She didn't say a word but ate in complete silence. Endymion wished he could hear her laugh again. After a while, he started speaking to break the stillness.

"My name's Endymion," he said. He considered adding, "What's yours?" but thought it would be assumed. She looked at him with a smile, tilting her head to one side as if she was trying to understand what he was saying. For a moment, the head tilt and the expression on her face reminded him of Scut, the dog who helped the shepherd in one of the neighboring crofts. Scut cocked his head the same way when spoken to in words more complex than the sheep herding commands he knew.

Endymion had asked his mother why they didn't have a dog. She had explained that dogs, while they could be helpful if you had a large herd, were expensive if they were well trained.

He flushed. He couldn't believe that he was comparing, even just in his head, this exquisite young woman to a shepherd's dog. Her smile broadened when she saw the pink rise in his cheeks.   To cover his blush, Endymion blurted out, "Endymion Silas Poimen, I come from the village down the mountain."

She reached out, picked up the piece of sheep cheese from his meal wrap, and took a delicate bite.

T hey ate in silence. Endymion lost himself looking at the young woman. His gaze lingered on her, drinking in the sight—until she glanced up, and he looked away, blushing again. She didn't seem to mind. She appeared to be studying him with as much interest.

She was small. Sitting across from Endymion, delicately chewing on the bread and cheese from his meager meal, she made him feel vast and ungainly. But there was no mistaking her for a child. In addition to the maturity of her face, which made him feel like she must be at least the same age as himself, he felt like graceful shapes were stirring beneath the flowing fabric of her green and brown cloak.

Endymion knew one thing that was in his mother's secret chest. When he was a child, Helen had once carefully removed a small, masterfully fashioned dollhouse from her trunk and shown it to him. It was a memory of her youth. She had shown it to him as a treasure—never to be touched, certainly not to be played with—but rather to be admired from afar. She didn't show him any dolls with it; it was an enchanting empty home, just waiting for someone to move in. When she put it away, he had felt regret, and he'd often thought of asking to see it again but never dared.

As Endymion glanced again at the young woman sitting across from him, he recalled how finely crafted and flawless the tiny fixtures and furniture had been in that delicate miniature house. He was looking at something equally exquisite and perfect—and for a moment, he forgot to breath.

When he could no longer hold his breath and the silence became unbearable, he started talking.

"I wonder what language you speak," he said. By this

point, he had concluded that the young woman's silence was due to his words being in a tongue unfamiliar to her.

She looked at him again, her face intelligent and curious. Her green eyes seemed to look straight through him—like a fresh green shoot breaking through spring soil.

Endymion leaned forward, focused on her bright, friendly face, and said, with deliberate slowness and as loudly as he could, "What language do you speak?"

T he young woman cupped both hands over her ears and, in a voice that was tinged with the sweet music that Endymion had heard in her laugh, said, "By the winds that fly across the mountain cliffs, I'm not deaf." She shook her head. "If I didn't understand your language, yelling wouldn't help. You might as well be trying to awaken the dead from their slumber."

Endymion's mouth dropped open. "I thought you couldn't understand me," he said plaintively.

"And that was your notion of a solution?" Her bright green eyes looked up at him, narrowing with interest. She put one finger on her lower lip. "I thought you a clever one, young Endymion Silas Poimen, but perhaps daft suits you better."

"Young?" said Endymion, arching his eyebrows. "You can't be much, if any, older than me."

"I may," said the young woman, her lips curling faintly upward, "Or I may not. We Wee Folk may not age the same as you Móra." She looked him challengingly in the eye. "Some might say the measure of age lies in its acts."

"Wee Folk!" said Endymion. "I thought so!"

"Aren't you a wily one, and make no mistake," she said. "Did you figure that out all by yourself?" She shook her head. "It's your people, you Móra, that call us that. I said it only to help you along."

As she spoke, her cloak slipped open a little, letting Endymion see her body as something other than a draped form for the first time. She was wearing the linen tunic he had seen before and a skirt. Both were woven in vivid patterns, contrasting with the subtle shades of the hooded garment. There was an image in the shadowed hollow of her tunic, just where the fabric met the skin, seemingly etched there in ink. A flower—he recognized it as the fire lily. He felt himself staring.

She sensed the stare. She flushed. "I've just the one," she said. Endymion didn't know what she meant. "I haven't earned any more," she continued.

Endymion looked up and caught her eye. She broke the gaze almost shyly, which surprised him.

"It's late," she said. She glanced up at the sun, which had moved well past its midday mark. "My mother will be wondering where I am." She got to her feet and started to walk away.

"But," said Endymion. "Will you come back? Will I see you again? What's your name? What do I call you?"

"Call me the wind.

Call me the mountain.

Call me the flower that blooms after the fire."

She met Endymion's eyes across the grass as she concluded, "Call me Lily."

THE WEE FOLK

That night, as the family broke their evening fast, Endymion wondered how to get his mother to speak of the Wee Folk without stirring her temper. Helen usually didn't need much prompting. She loved to tell stories and speak of things outside Woolfold in the Dell. Most of the time, it was easy to get her to talk about things beyond sheep-tending and herding. The last few nights had been an exception.

They ate around the table, the fire's comforting glow lighting the meal. Endymion's mother had prepared the customary shepherd's stew. She varied it when different ingredients were available. Still, a bowl of stew simmering over the fire was their usual evening meal.

Endymion had learned to cook a little and sometimes helped, but it was usually Helen who prepared the meals.

Endymion's father couldn't cook at all. Helen liked to say that he was the only man she knew who could burn a pot of water.

"Mother," Endymion said, "tell us a story." Endymion's father looked up curiously.

"Of course, dear," said Helen with a widening smile. "What story do you want to hear? What about *The Man Who Pulled the Moon from the Sky?* Or *The Deliverance of Death's Daughter?*"

"One I haven't heard before," Endymion said carefully. "Maybe something about the Wee Folk? Or fairy fruit?"

The corners of Helen's smile slipped downward toward a frown. "Endymion," she said. "We talked about this."

"I just want a story," said Endymion, "like you always used to tell me."

Helen's face grew thoughtful. "There is the tale of Sir

Branoc the Brooder," she said. "I don't think I've told you that one before."

"That sounds grand," said Endymion excitedly. He was pleased with how his strategy was working.

"Ewan," said Helen, "throw another log on the fire." Her smile returned. "After we're done eating, we're going to spin tales by the fireplace, just like we used to."

Endymion's father, his bowl empty, got up from the table and moved to the hearth in silence to tend to the blaze. Endymion stood and began clearing the table.

Helen's smile broadened. "Isn't this nice," she said.

Ewan sat on one side of the fireplace, Endymion on the other, and Helen between them, in the place of honor reserved for storytelling. Her face glowed in the firelight as she began. Her voice slipped into the sing-song tone Endymion knew so well.

"Now," she began, "in the days of old—before the land was called Liamec, long before the reign of our good king Twilight—the man who would become our first king, Liam the first, landed his ships on the coast near where Ardstead now stands."

"I haven't heard this one before," Endymion whispered eagerly across the flickering firelight to his father.

"Shhh," said Helen, raising one finger to her lips with theatrical flair. Endymion looked down at the rushes lining the floor.

"Now Liam had been granted the lands of Liamec by his father, but he and his men knew nothing of its virtues, secrets, or dangers, so Liam established a camp on the hill above a coastal fishing village, which would one day become the city of Ardstead." Helen frowned before continuing. "Of course, some say Liam's father had no authority to give away the land, as people already lived there—but that didn't trouble Liam or his men."

"Whose would it be if it wasn't King Liam's?" asked Endymion, surprised.

"Some say the land belongs to those who live on it—not to any king or ruler," Helen said gently, "But this is story time, not the floor of the Athenian assembly. We're not here to discuss politics." She repeated the finger to the lips in the shushing gesture.

Helen continued, "Anyway, Liam sent his knights out in

different directions to scout the countryside and learn what would be needed to establish control over the land.

"One among them was Sir Branoc the Brooder—though he had not yet earned the "Brooder" part of his title and was simply known as Sir Branoc at the time. He was a bold young knight, eager to prove his worth and eager to do his best for his lord."

With a sharp crack, a knot in a log burst open within the fire, scattering sparks. Endymion drew back a little to avoid an ember.

H elen resumed her story, "Some knights and their retinues went east and some south from the king's camp. Branoc set out to the west. He took a mapmaker and a scribe to chart the king's new territory, and a small troop of men to help persuade the locals their lands now belonged to the kingdom of Liamec.

"There were roads and villages, though nothing so civilized as we have now. The people spoke differently then—they used the old Hellenic tongue. Branoc and his men had trouble convincing the folk they met that they were now subject to Liam." She shook her head. "People can be so stubborn."

"But they did," said Endymion.

"Eventually," said Helen. "After one particularly contentious discussion—during which Branoc lost several men—he was feeling somewhat despondent. He trotted slowly down the road, debating whether to turn back and report his recent setback to his king, when he chanced upon a Sidhe woman standing by the roadside."

"Sidhe?" asked Endymion, frowning slightly.

"That's what they used to call the Wee Folk, back in the land across the sea where Liam and his men came from," said Helen.

"Why didn't they just call them the Wee Folk, like we do?" asked Endymion.

"Maybe they called them that as well," said Helen, with a flicker of annoyance. "Now, are you going to let me tell my story?"

Ewan looked back and forth from his wife to his son, following the exchange with great interest.

"Sorry," said Endymion in an embarrassed whisper,

shrinking back a little in his seat.

"The woman hailed Branoc in his own tongue. Intrigued, he urged his horse toward her." Helen stared intently into the crackling heart of the fire, as if reading the story in the flames. "Now, Branoc knew the tales of the Wee Folk that were told in his land; that they were tricky and could not be trusted, but also that they had great power and could wield mighty magics. He clutched his knife hilt, not because he thought a weapon would be much use against fae witchery, but because it was wrought iron, and he'd heard iron kept the Fae folk at bay."

"'How do you speak my tongue, woman?' he asked. The woman laughed. Branoc looked at her and, for a moment, couldn't tell if he was looking at a young woman or an older one —hearing an old crone's cackle or the lilting laugh of a maid."

"'Branoc,' she said—omitting any honorific or polite address—'I offer you a gift.' And she drew from somewhere behind herself a golden fruit that caught the last light of day, and held it out to him."

Endymion watched his mother. This was how he knew her best—lost in a story, while he sat quietly and listened. When she told a story, she seemed to disappear into it, and he would become caught in the tale as well. Firelight and shadows from the hearth danced across her face.

"'What is it?' asked Branoc, eyeing the fruit with suspicion.

"'It is a fae fruit,' said the woman. 'You may think of it as a golden apple.'

"'I will not eat of your fairy fruit,' said Branoc. 'I know the stories—they say I'll be lost in Fairyland, never to return and serve my king.'

"The woman shook her head. 'This is not that fruit,' she said calmly. 'This one gives the strength of ten—and no warrior who eats it can be defeated in battle.'

"Branoc's suspicions returned. 'Why would you offer me such a thing?' he asked. 'I come to claim these lands for King Liam and to establish his control over your people.'

"The woman shook her head. 'The Hellenes are not my people; they were merely earlier invaders,' she said. 'And, if the lands are to be under your king's control, it is better that the battles end quickly and fewer lives have their threads cut by the fates.'

"Branoc thought for a moment, then he reached down and took the fruit. As he took a bite, he felt the truth of what the woman had said. He felt his body flooding with power. 'Woman,' he said, 'you've done me—and your future king—a great service.' He pulled his sword from its sheath and brandished it toward the sky. 'My king,' he called out, 'the lands shall be yours!'"

Helen stirred, as if waking from a dream, and looked at

her son and husband. She nodded when she saw how attentive they both looked.

"Sir Branoc continued his journey. At first, the fae fruit served him well—for his strength truly was as the strength of ten. No one could stand against him and his men. The lands to the west of Liam's camp on the hill above the fishing village were soon offering their fealty to their new king." Helen paused, thoughtful. "You know, of course," she said, "that *Ard* is an old word for hill, and *Stede* means camp. A fitting name."

Endymion nodded as if everyone knew this. If he interrupted with a question, the end of the story might be delayed. "What happened to Branoc next?" he asked.

"He went south," said Helen. "He tried to extend his lord's control over the lands south of the coast. All was well—until the trickery of the Fae folk became clear, and the true nature of the golden apple revealed itself."

Helen continued, her voice slipping into a lilting rhythm. "With each battle, after each victory, doubt began to sprout in Branoc like a seed in the spring. At first, it was minor twinges. It was not just about the battles, but the lives he took and the lands he claimed. Did this opponent really need to die? Was that action of his men justified? He started questioning the very purpose of his mission. Did Liam really have the right to these lands? Were they wrong to be taking them from the current inhabitants?"

Helen shook her head. "The doubts grew until Branoc could no longer fight. His strength never wavered, and most thought his courage never did either. Still, some called his stepping down a failure of mettle rather than of morals. Anyway, it was as if the golden fruit had planted a seed of hesitation in him—one that grew until his soul leafed into a tree of uncertainty and doubt.

"It was at this time that he acquired the name of Branoc the Brooder, for he grew quiet and began to distance himself from Liam's other knights.

"Branoc lost favor with his lord. He retired and settled down to an uneventful life in Ardstead. Eventually, it is said he took up the tonsure and donned the habit of the first monastery established in the kingdom of Liamec."

"And the fairy woman?" asked Endymion, taking the chance that a brief interruption might escape notice.

"The Fae folk never gift a gift without a catch," said Helen. "In a single stroke—with one sweet bite—the fae woman seeded doubt in one of Liam's strongest knights." She frowned. "Of course, some say the doubt was already in him—and it didn't help in the long run. The kingdom of Liamec is as we know it now. In the end, the rest of Liam's men prevailed.

"And so it was," said Helen. This was her parting token when finishing a story. Endymion had heard it many times when he was younger, though not as many times as she had said it. Helen's stories had often been used to send him to sleep, so some of the times she had said it, it had been whispered to a boy already dreaming.

E ndymion spent the next morning practicing with his sling from his high seat above the sheep grazing below. He loaded a stone and spun the sling several times before releasing each shot. If he fired the rocks in quick succession, he would run out too fast.

When he climbed down from the escarpment, Lily was waiting for him.

"Are you ready to slay an ogre yet?" she asked him, her radiant smile almost stopping his heart.

"A weasel, maybe," he said, looking down at the ground lest she notice him staring.

"I brought my part of our noontide meal," said Lily, holding out her fabric-wrapped bundle.

Endymion raised his eyes from the ground to her face. It didn't take much—she stood closer to his heart than his height. The fact that she had said "Our meal" made him feel a warm glow, though he tried to keep this from his features.

They sat together again in the warm noonday sun, across from each other next to the stream, with their food spread out on the fabric wraps between them. Endymion took a bite or two of Lily's bread and cheese before picking up the fruit. He held it out to her.

"My mother says …" he hesitated. He'd been about to say something about fairy fruit carrying a trap, but he paused, realizing how that might sound. "My mother says," he repeated, "That fae fruit holds power—and can do things to you."

Lily laughed. Her laugh blended once more into the stream's soft music and the voice of the wind blowing past the rocks above them. "Ay, that's what we do." There was nothing but openness and honesty in her warm smile. "We lure innocent shepherds to their deaths by feeding them magical fruit."

Her cloak had fallen slightly open at the front, and again his eyes were drawn to the tattooed flower on her breast. It was just between the hollow of her throat and the edge of the colorful patterning on her linen tunic. The flower was bright red—clearly inked by the hand of an artist. The beauty of the depiction was striking.

He found himself caught in another prolonged stare. He shook his head, heat rushing to his cheeks, and turned to look at the water running past in the little brook.

Trying to steer toward safer ground, Endymion asked a question that had been weighing on his heart.

"Why are you here, Lily?" he asked. "Why are you sharing this meal with me?"

For the first time, Lily's smile wavered. The corners of her mouth—where her smile had bloomed—fell. It reminded Endymion of his mother's reaction to his asking about the Wee Folk the night before. "Well, that's a fine how-do-you-do," she said. "Would you rather that I wasn't here?"

Endymion panicked. "No!" he blurted out, "That's not what I meant—I just …"

Lily's smile returned. There was an edge of playfulness in it this time. "What did you mean?" she asked.

"I meant …" said Endymion, hesitating as he tried to figure out what to say. "Why me? How did you find me, and why would you choose me to share your meal with?"

"Well," said Lily thoughtfully, "That's easy to answer in some ways and harder in others." She paused, then nodded. Endymion noticed the way her copper plaits bounced with the motion. "I'll start with the easy part.

"I heard the flute first." She looked up into Endymion's eyes, and his chest fluttered. *If I don't stop reacting to her like this, my heart might give out*, he thought. Lily continued, "It was special, like nothing I'd ever heard before." She frowned. "My father plays the pipe, and he's very good, I have to say." She shook her head. "It's not that you're better; it was just very different." She met his gaze again, the playful smile back in its place on her red lips. "I repeat: you're not better."

"What does your music sound like?" asked Endymion.

"After that," said Lily, seeming to ignore his question, "I hope you don't mind, but I looked into your pouch. That carving —it's meant to be the lone ewe, the humble one, isn't it?"

"Urania," said Endymion.

"I think you caught a little bit of her in it."

Endymion started to say something else, but Lily kept talking.

"About our music?" she said. "I could sing you something if you'd like. I don't have an instrument here."

Endymion nodded. "I think I would like that," he said.

L ily cocked her head to one side as if thinking. Endymion guessed she was choosing what song to sing. The wind brushing by the rocks overhead and the stream's gentle sighing seemed to already be singing. To Endymion, it felt like an ode to Lily's beauty. He started to feel a deep sense of contentment. It unnerved him how much joy he felt in this moment. It was like his happiness was balanced on a knife's edge and could be taken away at any time.

"You're beautiful," he said softly. So softly it was as if he hadn't meant her to hear it at all.

For a moment, Endymion thought that the red from her lips and the red color of her hair had joined in the middle, coloring her already rosy cheeks an even prettier shade of pink. It was simply that it was her turn to flush. She looked at the ground.

Almost as softly as he had said his words, she replied, "You're not so bad yourself."

Surprised, Endymion said, "Me? I'm just me; there's nothing special about me." He studied her face again, still turned toward the ground, and said, "But, you? You're magical."

She looked up, the fading flush still coloring her cheeks, and said, "Yes, I am, aren't I?"

She shook her head as if to get past something silly or nonsensical. "This is a song that mothers sing to their babies to put them to sleep." She started singing in a soft, hushed voice that grew stronger until it filled the Dell with a captivating sound like sheep's milk filling the bowl when Endymion's mother began to make cheese.

Endymion lay back on the grass and listened.

The words were strange to him—her own language, no

doubt. But he felt he could hear the meaning coming through the melody and the voice. An image came to him: a woman who looked like Lily, leaning over a cradle. He felt like he was the babe in the cradle, and he could feel acres of warmth pouring down onto him from the image in his mind's eye and the sounds bathing his ears.

The voices of the wind rustling the leaves of the mountain trees and bushes and the gentle laughing of the brook were still there, blending seamlessly with the words of Lily's song.

Endymion drifted off to sleep.

A voice stirred Endymion from his peace-lulled slumber. The voice made him feel peaceful and rested for a moment, but as his brain struggled to rise from its torpor, a note of insistence in it rang a warning bell in his mind. It was Lily's voice, saying his name.

"Endymion Silas Poimen," she said in hushed urgency. "You must rise now. The time to sleep is past."

Endymion opened his eyes. Lily was standing over him. It was the first time he had looked up at her from below. The angle didn't diminish her beauty. He started to rise groggily. She put her hand on his chest and stilled his upward motion gently. The rocks of the escarpment behind her framed her copper plaits.

"Carefully, Endymion," she said, her voice just above a whisper. "You have listened to the fae song and eaten of the fairy fruit. You have been asleep for one hundred years. Your body will need to recover from the stresses of time."

Endymion blinked. He looked around as much as his supine position allowed. "A hundred years?" he asked, "But you look the same."

Lily nodded. "We Fae folk do not age as you mortals do. When I met you, I was already one hundred years old." She smiled at him. "Everything you knew is gone. You will have no choice but to come and live with us Wee Folk in Fairyland."

"But," said Endymion, "you're dressed the same."

Lily's smile turned to a frown, though Endymion thought he saw the smile staying hidden behind the knotted brow.

"Are you questioning my wardrobe choices?" she said indignantly.

Endymion rose to a seated position. Her hand stayed gently on his chest, though it didn't try to stop his motion this time. He looked from side to side.

"Everything looks the same," he said. "The bushes and trees haven't grown."

"Well …" said Lily.

At that moment, Urania bleated out her displeasure at something. Endymion turned his head toward the sound, though the rock escarpment blocked his view of the sheep. It was his turn to frown.

"What's going on?" he asked.

Lily began to laugh. Through his confusion, Endymion couldn't help but think that he had never heard a more delightful sound.

Endymion stood awkwardly, the grogginess of sleep slowing him. Lily looked up at him, the smile on her face warming his heart against his own instincts. He looked around. The sun had crept no more than a hand's breath across the sky. He couldn't have been asleep for more than the time it took to milk a ewe.

"You're a scoundrel," he said, though a smile was sneaking into his voice.

"I'm not a scoundrel," said Lily, "I'm fun."

Endymion started to laugh. The freshness of the afternoon, the pleasure of Lily's company, and the relief of not having outlived everything he knew built up in him. He laughed until his side started to ache. Lily smiled at him until he stilled.

"I'm glad you liked that one," she said, "I thought it was pretty good myself."

Endymion looked at her. "You aren't really a hundred years old?" he asked. He was surprised to find that there was a bit of a beseeching tone in his voice. He found himself waiting breathlessly for her answer.

Lily looked back at him. She scanned him from head to foot. Endymion felt himself start to warm under the scrutiny. "Nay," she said. "I would guess that I am not much older or younger than you are yourself." She nodded, "I have seen sixteen summers and winters come and go."

Endymion felt content. The warm late spring sun was shining down on the fresh grass, the sounds of the mountain filled the air around them, and every time he looked at Lily, he felt a surge of joy. "Thank you, Lily, for breaking bread with me," he said, "I've really been enjoying the time, and your presence makes this gorgeous day even more beautiful."

"A thing of beauty is a joy forever," said Lily. "Even if the day lasts just a moment, our memories of it can last our lifetimes."

Endymion nodded. What she said felt very right. He caught himself staring at her bright red lips again.

Lily looked up at him. "Would you like to kiss me?" she asked carefully.

Something in Endymion was trembling, though he kept himself still. "Is that a thing that could happen?" he asked.

"It is," said Lily, glancing down at the ground. "It is a thing that could happen."

Endymion lowered himself on one knee and leaned toward Lily. He felt her breath warm on his face. She moved closer, and their lips touched.

Endymion was lost—lost in a world of sensations he had never known. The rustling leaves and murmuring brook were still there—but they faded beside the heat burning on his lips. It was warmth and intimacy and wetness and sweetness and fire all at once.

Lily's lips pressing against his burned into him. He felt like the fire lily his lips were touching wasn't the flower but rather a burning ember from an actual fire.

Her mouth opened just a little, and he felt the tip of her tongue questing carefully through. He met it with his own, and the fire leapt higher as their tongue tips brushed against each other.

Endymion opened his eyes. Lily's green eyes were already open. He felt like he was diving into green pools of water. The emerald depths lured him onward.

Lily's breath burned hot and sweet against his cheek—another facet of the flower. He wanted to breathe it and nothing else, forever.

They pulled apart, both breathing a little heavily. Endymion stood. Lily looked at the sun.

"Oh," she said huskily, "I have to go. My mother will be wondering where I am."

"Can't you stay just a little bit longer?" asked Endymion, holding out his hand toward her.

Lily eyed the hand as if it were some strange creature. It hung there, nearly at her eye level. "No," she said. "I don't want to worry her." She hurriedly packed up what was left of her food bundle.

Endymion watched her, admiring every move she made —even as he regretted each one, knowing it carried her farther away.

"Tomorrow?" he said carefully, hopefully, wistfully.

"Tomorrow," said Lily over her shoulder with a smile, stepping lightly through the grass toward the edge of the clearing.

E ndymion spent the morning of the next day working on his carving of Urania. He was encouraged by Lily's recognition of his shaping as the hindmost sheep. Each stroke of the knife was deliberate, each one meant to draw out Urania's heart. Endymion once again cursed his choice of the soft-grained wood.

Lily was waiting when he climbed down from the rocks. His heart gave a sudden leap, though he did his best to appear calm.

As they opened their food bundles, Endymion kept sneaking glances at the Wee Folk woman to make sure he wasn't dreaming her.

"How are your lips so red?" he asked, then flushed and shook his head at himself.

Lily laughed. She didn't seem to mind whatever impropriety Endymion had thought was in the question. "Are they?" she replied, smiling at him.

Endymion nodded. "They're redder than anyone's I've ever seen," he said. "I didn't think lips could be so red."

"Women in my village stain their lips to give them color. My sister uses a lighter, more rosy shade. I like the dark red, like the fire lily—because of my name, of course." Lily smiled.

To Endymion, the moment felt like a fleeting treasure—a chance to gaze at her lips without shame. He tried to etch the image into his memory, as he had etched Urania's face into the wood.

Lily continued, "Don't the women in your village color their lips?"

Endymion furrowed his brow in thought. "I don't think so, no," he said. "At least, I've never noticed it." He took a breath.

"So tell me," he said eagerly, leaning closer. "You mentioned your mother—and a sister." He grinned, unable to hide his excitement. "How many are there in your family, and where do you live?"

Lily paled and drew back slightly, an unfamiliar expression flickering across her face. "I'm not supposed to talk about that," she said, faltering.

Endymion was puzzled for a moment, then he thought he understood. "Oh," he said carefully. "I'm sorry—I guess I shouldn't have asked where your village is."

Lily shook her head. "It's all right," she said. "I can talk about my family. It's just that we've been told since we were wee that we shouldn't talk to outsiders about where we live." She frowned. "There were troubles," she said, giving him a searching look. "Before I was born."

L ily looked up at Endymion, her eyes losing all trace of defense. "I have one sister," she said. "In your language, I suppose you'd call her Blossom." She hesitated for a moment before continuing. "She's older—she's the pretty one."

"Wait," said Endymion, confusion casting a shadow across his features, "The pretty one? How could she be the pretty one? I can't imagine anyone prettier than you."

"You'll understand if you ever meet her," said Lily. "My family calls me 'The Bear' because I'm so big and ungainly." She frowned. "Blossom is trim, light, and graceful as a swan. I'm a head taller than my sister and my mother—and easily as tall as my father."

"Lily," said Endymion, looking at the ground though he wanted to meet her eyes. "You're the most radiant thing I've ever seen in my life."

Endymion wanted to say more—something about how the afternoon sunlight made her hair glow like copper, or how her smile made his heart beat too fast. But the words got stuck in his tangled tongue.

Lily was silent, but when Endymion finally looked up and met her gaze, she was smiling at him.

"My mother is the village Herbmother, and my father the Greenwarden."

Endymion shook his head. "I don't know what those things are," he said.

"You don't have a Herbmother in your village?" asked Lily. "She prepares medicinal plants and knows the remedies for whatever ails the village."

"Ah," said Endymion. "I suppose we do. Our cunning woman, Marjoram, does that for us." He thought for a moment that Marj might like being called Herbmother. He continued, "And, what's a Greenwarden?"

"A Greenwarden?" said Lily. "My father listens to the forests and tells the people what the trees and plants need." She tilted her head to one side. "He also collects leaves, roots, and fungi for my mother's remedies."

Endymion noticed Lily's hands. She was twisting her fingers together—the same way he did when his feelings were overflowing. His heart surged. It wasn't just him, overcome by her presence—she felt it too.

The next day, Clio joined Endymion and Lily as they broke their noonday fast. The sheep, the most curious of the flock, came nosing into the sward between Lily and Endymion. She sniffed at the food laid out on their wraps. Lily laughed, and Endymion caught his breath—her laugh hit him like a warm wind. He smiled, and simply listened.

"Silly sheep," said Lily. "That's not sheep food." She put her hand up and touched the sheep gently on the side of her face. She started speaking to Clio in another language. The lilting sound of her own tongue made her voice seem even more enchanting. Clio lowered her head toward Lily as if she were bowing. She started pushing forward against Lily's hand.

"Clio," said Endymion, "calm down." He started to get to his feet, worried the sheep would push against Lily roughly enough to knock her over. Clio looked at Endymion, as if to say he didn't understand what was going on, and then she lay down on the grass beside Lily.

Endymion sat back down. "Huh," he said, looking at the sheep, who had started chewing on some easy-to-reach grass while resting her back against Lily's side. "She doesn't usually lie down," he continued.

"She must like me better than you," said Lily, a mischievous glint in her eye. "Maybe she thinks I'd make a better shepherd than you."

"Oh," said Endymion challengingly, "and what would you do differently than me if you had the tending of my herd?"

Lily said, with complete seriousness, "I'd teach the sheep to dance—and, name them after the stars, not the muses." She looked pensive for a moment. "She might be Capella, for instance."

"She's Clio," said Endymion. "I think she likes being Clio." He ruffled the tuft of wool between her ears.

Clio bleated, looking at Lily. Endymion chose to interpret it as agreeing with him. Though most likely, Lily thought the sheep was agreeing with her.

Endymion leaned back and looked at the Wee Folk woman. He wondered how it was that someone so small had made her way into such a big space in his heart—so quickly.

THUDWHACK

For the next several days, Lily joined Endymion for their midday meal. Endymion rose early each morning to get the sheep on the trail before sunrise. If another shepherd reached their meadow first, he might not see Lily that day. It never occurred to him to go to a different valley to graze the sheep.

His parents were impressed, thinking he was finally taking his shepherding seriously.

In a way, he was.

Lily and Endymion discussed life, each other's families, and the sheep. They were careful to stay away from anything controversial. Endymion, especially, never mentioned anything about his mother's and, by extension, the other villager's attitudes toward the Wee Folk.

*　*　*

"Lily," said Endymion one day as they lay on their backs in the warm sun, listening to the brook gurgle its peaceful song, "What would I do if you stopped coming?"

Lily turned her head toward him and smiled. "You'll just do whatever it was you used to do before I started meeting you," she said.

"I can't," said Endymion. "I couldn't." He shook his head. "Promise me that you'll always come?"

Lily frowned. "Always is an awfully long time. It's such a long time for such a small word." Her frown deepened, and Endymion found his gaze caught on the slight crease in her brow. "I shouldn't tell you this," she murmured, "but you could try to find me."

"How?" asked Endymion. "I have no idea where to look."

Lily looked at the ground. "I never give my trust to anyone

for fear it might be broken," she said. "If I trust you, you won't break that trust, will you, Endymion Silas Poimen?"

"Never," said Endymion. "If you give me your trust, I will hold it like a precious thing. I could never break such a precious thing."

Lily lifted her eyes to Endymion's face. He saw a trace of worry there. "There's a marked trail." She pointed to one of the scraggly mountain trees on one side of the glade. "That's where it begins."

Endymion looked. The tree seemed no different from the rest. He shook his head. "I don't see anything," he said.

"If you look about halfway up the trunk," said Lily, changing the direction she was pointing to about the middle of the tree. "You can see a ring in the bark around the tree that's a different color. That marks the trail to my village." She shook her head again and continued, "And with that, I've told you exactly what I wasn't supposed to. Who's under the spell of the fairy fruit now?"

When Endymion came down from his rocky seat the next day, he reached out his hand toward Lily, who was waiting there for him. She took his large, rough fingers in her own—delicate and much smaller. "I have a riddle for you," he said. "I've been working on it all morning."

"Oh," said Lily, a glimmer starting to glow in the corner of her green eyes. "I like riddles."

"All right," said Endymion nervously. "It might be a challenging one."

"Come then," said Lily, the glow intensifying, "Let's see what you can do, shepherd."

He paused, then asked, "What has no wings yet soars higher than any bird?"

Lily frowned. "The sun?" she said.

Endymion shook his head. "It may be higher than the birds, but it doesn't soar—and it's not the answer I was thinking of." He let go of Lily's hand reluctantly, moved over near the creek, and started spreading out his meal wrap.

Lily moved to do the same with her meal. "The clouds?" she ventured.

Endymion shook his head again and took a seat on the grass across from Lily. "Like the sun, it doesn't soar—and again, not what I was thinking of." He looked thoughtful for a moment, then continued, "Anyway, a good riddle has a bit of a twist or a trick to it." He nodded. "This one is tailored just for you."

"It could be the sky itself, but that has the same problem," said Lily. Endymion found his gaze tracing the slight furrow that formed in her brow.

"Do you yield?" he said.

"Never," said Lily. "We Wee Folk may be smaller than you

Móra—but we are strong and resilient. We never yield. Not while there remains breath within us—never."

They resumed eating, Lily in silence, Endymion lost in the depths of the furrow.

"Móra," said Endymion after a while. "You used that word before. What does it mean?"

Lily shook her head. "It means little more than 'Other.' It's just our word for anyone not of the Wee Folk. Your kind."

For some reason, this answer made Endymion a little downcast. He went back to eating, his movements subdued.

"Mayhap," said Lily after a while, "I do not yield, as that is something the Wee Folk never do, but mayhap it might be wise for me to allow you to believe you've won. Just for the sake of your morale."

"So," Endymion smiled, "you want to hear the answer?"

Lily nodded, a frown battling with a trace of a smile at the corners of her mouth.

"The thing that has no wings yet soars higher than any bird," said Endymion. He paused. "Is my heart when I come down from my ledge at noontide and see you waiting for me."

T he next day, Lily didn't come. Endymion's heart skipped a beat when he climbed down from his perch—and didn't see her. For a moment, it seemed to stop altogether. Then, reluctantly, it started again.

Maybe she's just late, he thought. *I'm sure if I just wait a little while, she'll be here soon.* But his heart told him otherwise.

After waiting for what felt like an eternity, Endymion could wait no longer. Somehow—though he couldn't say how—he knew something was wrong. He packed everything into his pocket and went first to check on the sheep.

Endymion looked Calliope in the eye. "Cally," he said firmly, "You're going to have to keep them all together in the meadow."

Calliope gave a thoughtful bleat, as if she understood.

He wasn't too worried. They would stay put unless something startled them. Stilll, he couldn't shake the feeling he was letting his family down, leaving the sheep in the vale unprotected. But he knew he had to find Lily.

He made his way over to the weathered tree that Lily had pointed out the other day. The ring blaze around the tree was subtle. If he hadn't known what to look for, he never would have seen it. It just looked like a patch of bark in a slightly different shade. It was almost as if the tree had been instructed to grow its bark lighter at that height.

Endymion stood by the weathered tree and looked beyond it. Again, if he hadn't known to look here, the trail would have been invisible. As it was, when he looked carefully, he could make out faint signs that people had traveled this way, and not far away, he saw another tree with a similar blaze at about the same height.

Endymion started down the trail, his heart beating so that it felt like it was trying to pound its way out of his chest. The way became easier to see as he moved along, not because the signs grew clearer, but because his eyes grew used to them. He quickened his pace, urgency building with every breath.

The trail led on and on through the mountains. Each step took Endymion farther from the paths he knew. Though the sun was shining and it was only the start of a lovely mountain afternoon, Endymion felt like some darkness was leeching the warmth from the day's light.

He knew there was something wrong. Not just something wrong—something wrong with Lily. She was in trouble. The thought made him hurry his steps even more, though he made sure not to lose sight of the trail. The path was cleverly placed, cutting through narrow gaps in cliffs and finding dry paths through mountain bogs that would have been impossible to see without it.

The trail climbed westward through the mountains, up and down ridges and slopes. Endymion was soon certain he'd never find his way home without the markings. However, now that he knew how to read them, the tree blazes and, in some places, piled stone cairns were consistent and clear.

With nothing to occupy his mind except worry, Endymion began to wonder what was beyond the Etenies mountains. His village, Woolfold in the Dell, was really only in the foothills. Even after all this walking, he could still see the snow-capped peaks ahead, rising in the west. He knew that if you sailed along the coast, leaving Liamec behind in the east, you would run into other lands. His mother had mentioned Aquitaine and Galicia. The names didn't mean much to him, however.

Endymion shook his head. It didn't matter. He was never going to walk far enough to reach another kingdom, and even if he did walk that far, perhaps the fabled land of Fairyland was between here and there. Certainly, Lily's village lay somewhere in that direction.

Endymion was just beginning to wonder how Lily made it this far each morning to meet him for their noontide repast when a break in the trail cut short his thoughts.

Something big—big, and with no interest in hiding its passage—had crashed across the Wee Folk trail, leaving deep ruts behind.

Endymion swallowed. The creature that left those ruts wouldn't be interested in riddles.

W hatever had cut across the path clearly had no interest in concealing which way it was going. The direction of travel on the new cross trail was obvious. Slender trees had been broken completely in half. Branches lay snapped, and the earth was scuffed as if something massive had shuffled through.

Endymion set off down the new path, almost running. The trail was easy to follow, though he tempered his speed a little not wanting to charge headfirst into whatever had made it. The track continued further into the mountains.

After he'd been following it for a while, the trail led into an alpine marsh. Endymion hesitated for a moment, unsure if it would be as easy to follow the track with the swampy area's lower vegetation and fewer trees. Then he saw the imprints left in the muck and loam of the swamp by the thing he was tracking.

He followed the signs, taking care not to get too deeply mired in the mud himself. The traces of whatever creature he was following made it easy to tell where the mud was deep and where it was firmer.

Endymion paused. In one firm patch of peat, the creature had left a clear print. It startled him—but not entirely. It was a bare human-looking footprint—twice the size of any such print he had ever seen before. He'd suspected this from the beginning. There weren't too many things out here in the mountains that were big enough not to fear anything—and not to care what might track or follow them. An ogre was one of those few. Endymion was tracking an ogre.

He thought about this for a moment. He didn't know too much about ogres; certainly nothing first-hand. He knew they were big, mean, and ate human flesh. They lived alone. He believed it was because they couldn't stand the presence of others—not even their own kind.

One thing he did know: you didn't track ogres. They tracked you if you were unlucky. If you knew where one was, you went the other way.

Endymion let out a breath. Then, breaking the one rule he knew about ogres, he raced across the firm peat and up the slope beyond, tracking it.

A fter a while, the trail merged into an older track. This wasn't a cleared footpath, like the ones Endymion followed each morning from his village into the mountains, or a blazed trail like the one he'd been taking toward the Wee Folk village. Instead, it was an animal track—created by an animal that habitually took the same route, wearing down the vegetation with each passage. It had been cleared, however, by something huge, and Endymion was sure that this was a track the ogre used to travel to and from its nest.

Endymion paused. The clear, fresh trail he'd been following ended here. The ogre had turned onto its regular route and abandoned the rough push through the underbrush. He scanned the new track to see which way the creature had gone.

Based on how the underbrush was broken and trodden where the creature had merged onto its more familiar path, he picked a direction and continued.

The animal trail wound even further into the mountains. Without the sun to gauge direction by, Endymion would have lost his feeling for which way was east or west; as it was, he no longer had any clear sense of the way home.

Endymion eased his pace. He felt an urgency to follow the creature, but he didn't want to stumble on it unprepared. He crept carefully forward along the trampled trail.

He paused at the edge of a large clearing. A cliff face towered over the open space, and one side of it was walled by rock. There was a wide opening in the rock face, looking like a yawning mouth. Even from this distance, Endymion could sense the thick, fetid air seeping out of the cave beyond.

Bones littered the barren hollow's floor. Endymion didn't look closely, because he didn't want to see what kind of bones they were. But, even at a cursory glance, human skulls of all sizes were impossible to overlook.

Several other forest tracks led out of the rough break in the mountain vegetation. They led off in all directions. Endymion speculated that they were the ways the ogre went to hunt when he left his camp.

A large smoldering firepit was in the center of the clearing, between the edge of the track that Endymion had come down and the cave mouth. The firepit, ringed by rough stones, looked like it was repeatedly stirred to life and fed each evening.

But what made Endymion freeze in the shrubs at the edge of the clearing was the figure seated on a large rock by the smoldering firepit.

It was the ogre.

T he creature was enormous—as Endymion had expected. Its size was roughly what he had imagined, yet seeing it in person was more fearsome than any mental picture. Even seated, it loomed taller than Endymion would have been standing beside it. The rock it squatted on was so large Endymion would have struggled to climb it.

It was gigantic, naked, and filthy. Its form resembled a large, rough, unclothed man, though one who would stand ten feet tall if he stood an inch. Endymion made a conscious effort to avoid looking between its legs—where even a modicum of decency would have warranted a loincloth—but it was undeniably male.

A large tree branch, now a crude club, leaned against a boulder near where the creature was sitting. The simple expedient of breaking off branches on the business end of the club had left behind cracked, sharp stubs. They formed effective spikes, making the rough weapon look savagely deadly. That end of the branch was matted with brown stains that were unmistakably dried blood.

Endymion scanned the site carefully, desperate to spot something that might give him a hint as to Lily's fate.

There wasn't much else in the clearing. A pile of firewood, just broken, scraggly mountain trees, lay haphazardly. It looked like the creature had just pulled them from the ground and thrown them into a heap until it was ready to toss them onto the fire.

There were a few tree limbs that Endymion would have had trouble lifting, burned on one end, which looked like they might serve as crude fire pokers when the fire was blazing.

On one side of the clearing was the remains of a trader's

handcart. It was the sort of thing that a wandering merchant might pull into Woolfold's square on market day. The village market was an important event in Woolfold in the Dell, as it was one of the few times when the villagers might see people from outside the village. Endymion was surprised to see the wreckage this high up in the mountains. Perhaps the ogre, with its long legs, had a broad hunting range.

He spotted it. Near the firepit, atop a pile of rough burlap sacks, was one that had a pair of legs sticking out of it. Endymion recognized Lily's legs, clad in fitted leggings. His heart skipped a beat until he saw the legs shift. Lily was still struggling, futilely, to escape the confines of the burlap sack.

The ogre spoke.

E ndymion's heart leapt into his throat. For a moment, he thought the creature had detected him and was talking to him. Then he realized that it was talking to itself. He had a moment of surprise at the notion that it could speak at all.

"Day good," grunted the orge with satisfaction, glancing idly at the pair of legs still kicking at the end of the burlap sack.

Endymion felt rage building within him.

"Thudwhack, good hunter," said the monster, practically glowing with pride.

Endymion's anger simmered hot beneath his skin. It did surprise him, even through his rage, that the creature had a name for itself.

"Most time," said Thudwhack, "little ones hard catch."

Endymion's glare burned across the clearing at the creature.

Thudwhack eyed the burlap sack. "Little one head somewhere else," he said, rubbing his chin, "not watch."

Endymion fixed his stare on Thudwhack as he scratched his head, then studied his broken, dirty fingernail as if it held a secret.

"Little one pretty," said the ogre.

Endymion's fists clenched.

"Pretty... taste better."

Endymion realized he was about to break a tooth if he didn't stop gritting his teeth.

"Little ones say not eat them," Thudwhack said. "Little ones say Thudwhack big trouble eat little one."

The ogre visibly scoffed. "Every one say, 'Not eat me,'" he continued. "Deer think 'not eat me.'"

Endymion pulled back a little from the clearing, keeping

within earshot for now.

"Thudwhack, hungry?" asked the ogre of himself.

Endymion held his breath, waiting for the answer to this question. There had never been a question he had asked or heard asked in his life where the answer mattered more to him.

The ogre shook his head. "Eat time come later," he muttered.

Endymion turned and crept down the path until he was far enough away from the clearing that the ogre could not see or hear him. Then he started running down the track, every stride faster than the last.

Endymion ran. He ran like all the demons of hell were close at his heels. He ran like the golden carrot of the gods was being dangled in front of him. He ran down the broad animal track like he'd never run before.

He kept his eyes open for the place where the fresher track that he had followed here broke into the broad way that the ogre used more regularly. He had to ease his steps a little after that, as the trail was less clear. Still, he leapt from rock to rock, from solid-looking patches of ground in the swampy parts, over muddy puddles, always trying to increase his pace.

Endymion lived the life of a shepherd—up with the morning sun, outside almost the whole day, hiking up mountain trails and climbing rocks. Still, he wasn't used to this. When his body told him to stop, to ease up, to rest, he overrode it and kept running. His legs felt like lead, his breath came in ragged gasps, and his heart pounded in his chest, but he kept going.

As he ran, Endymion's thoughts were consumed by Lily —her hair, her lips, her eyes. He thought about the way her lips tasted when they kissed. They were shy about it, but they had kissed a few more times since that first time. He thought about how playful and clever she was. He almost cried when he thought about how she made fun of him sometimes. For some reason, at this moment, that felt like the best part.

When the fresh ogre track intersected with the blazed Wee Folk path, Endymion turned to the right, away from the direction that led back toward the dell where his sheep waited. For a moment, he had a flash of guilt about the sheep— abandoned and alone. Then, he had a vision of Calliope, Urania, and the rest munching idly on the green sward of the meadow, and he threw himself forward again.

Fortunately for Endymion, the Wee Folk path, with its blazes and thoughtful construction, was easy to follow, as he knew what to look for. It was lucky that the tree marks were clearly spotted, as Endymion's vision was starting to blur, and each gasping breath was producing a sharp pain in his chest.

After Endymion had run for what felt like forever, the trail broke into a large clearing. One side of the clearing was a timeless-looking wooden palisade overgrown with plants, including many vines blooming with colorful flowers. The wooden gates of the palisade were wide open. Several Wee Folk stood around the open space. They reacted with startlement when Endymion burst out of the trail-head.

"Móra," Endymion heard someone yell through the ringing in his ears. He ignored them and ran through the wooden gate. The path opened into a village square on the other side. The air smelled of damp bark and wildflowers.

The square was ringed by buildings unlike anything he had ever seen. They were bigger than the houses of his village, but more than that, they looked like they were grown rather than built. Some blended seamlessly into the mountain stone; others rose from massive trees, their trunks shaped as if coaxed into place.

The Wee Folk going about their business in the square stopped and stared at the stranger who had suddenly appeared in their midst.

"Lily," croaked Endymion as loudly as he could. He sank to his knees and then collapsed onto the cobbled stones of the square. The paving stone in front of his eyes seemed like it had some quartz or something in it, as it, along with the rest of the stones of the square, shimmered in the late afternoon sun.

The world blurred for Endymion and faded into darkness.

Endymion woke with a gasp. There was a sharp scent, like the smell of winter ice, stinging his nostrils. He opened his eyes to Lily's deep forest green ones gazing down at him. He was lost for a moment in the comforting emerald depths.

"Lily?" he murmured, feeling his head cradled in her lap. He breathed a sigh of contentment.

But it wasn't Lily. It was a stern-mouthed older Wee Folk woman with Lily's eyes. Endymion blinked, struggling to make sense of it.

"Drink this," she said gruffly, pulling something away from under his nose and rather roughly forcing a flask of something else into his mouth.

Endymion sputtered. Whatever was in the flask had a bitter taste, and it stung his lips. It did, however, wake him up further and make him feel alert. He pushed himself upright on the glittery cobblestones.

A circle of Wee Folk surrounded them, some with weapons drawn. Sitting, he was at eye level with most of them. The weapons were knives and short swords. Each blade glittered with the same mica-like glow as the cobblestones.

The woman he had been speaking to was seated cross-legged on the paving stones next to him. She looked like an older version of Lily, though she wasn't wearing the green-brown cloak that Lily always wore.

She stood. Endymion felt pierced through by those green eyes that looked just like Lily's. "Who are you, coming into our village uninvited, with my daughter's name on your lips?" she asked, her voice echoing off the glittering cobblestones.

Everything came back to Endymion in a rush. "Lily's in

trouble," he said urgently, his voice trembling. "An ogre who calls himself Thudwhack has her, and he's going to eat her if we don't rescue her."

The woman's eyes opened wide. "We?" she asked, but she nodded at some of the armed Wee Folk standing in the circle around them. Several of them urgently rushed off. Endymion's heart leapt, and he breathed a sigh of relief.

The woman busied herself with something on her belt. Endymion noticed that she had a wide belt with many small pouches attached to it. With a practiced motion, she pulled out a small, round pot of ointment.

Endymion started to rise to his feet. The armed Wee Folk who hadn't left tightened their grips on their weapons. Tension crackled, and Endymion checked his rise.

"You're not going anywhere," said the Wee Folk woman. She reached forward with the ointment pot and held it under his nose. Another smell, sickly sweet and overpowering, entered Endymion's nostrils. And once more, the world slipped away.

E ndymion shook off sleep reluctantly, lying on the green sward beneath the rocky outcrop in the meadow. Urania was licking his face. The memory of what had happened flooded into him, and he sat upright like a boy startled from a nightmare.

His head collided with Urania's with a thump. The startled sheep bolted.

"Ow," said Endymion, rubbing his head. "Sorry, Urania."

Endymion looked around. The sun was low. There was no sign that anything had happened—other than him eating his midday meal and sleeping too long. *Had it been a dream?*

He shook his head. *Of course not; it had all been too real.*

Endymion rose to his feet. The sun was beginning to set. If he wanted to get the sheep home, he'd better start now and hope for a clear sky and a bright moon, as well.

He thought again about what had happened and felt a surge of relief. Somehow, he knew that the Wee Folk had gotten to Thudwhack's cave in time. He knew that Lily was safe. The weight of worry lifted from his shoulders. He wasn't so sure about Thudwhack… but he didn't much care.

The sheep were all there. Endymion gathered them together and set Calliope in her lead position. She gave him a look filled with a combination of disappointment and pride. She was disappointed in him but proud she'd held the herd together during his dereliction of duty. Endymion gave her a carrot piece.

The sky was clear, and the moon was bright. The sheep knew the trail, and the walk went smoothly. As they neared Woolford, Endymion saw a lit lantern approaching on the trail.

It was Leland. "Endymion!" he called, when the light from his lantern caught his face.

Endymion's parents had gotten worried and called for help. Some of the villagers had turned out to search. They had to ring the church bells to let the searchers know that he'd been found. It took some time for them all to get the news and return.

Endymion, shamefaced, explained that he'd just fallen asleep on the grass and hadn't awoken until sunset. It was an embarrassing story, and he could feel a flush of warmth rising in his cheeks, but he knew he had to lie.

The truth, after all, would wake a slumbering dragon—and dragons do not wake gently.

The following morning, as soon as the sheep were spreading out into the meadow, Endymion went to look for the trail. He had no plan. He just knew he had try to find Lily, and make sure she was all right. Endymion was certain that the Wee Folk woman who had woken him in the village was Lily's mother. He hoped he could convince her that she had to let him see Lily.

The trail was gone. The blazes on the trees were simply not there anymore. There was no sign that anyone had ever traveled that way. It was like the traces had just disappeared. Endymion tried to follow the path by his memory of where it had been, but after the first tree, it was impossible to tell which one came next.

He returned to the clearing, disheartened. Urania sensed his distress and bleated at him consolingly. He scratched the tuft of wool atop her head.

Endymion tried to spend his morning carving. He attempted to practice with his sling. His flute didn't help. Nothing worked. He couldn't stop thinking about Lily. After a while, he just sat, his back to the rock of his escarpment, and brooded.

Lily didn't show up at noon. He wasn't surprised. The stern look on Lily's mother's face, not to mention the barely cloaked hostility from the other Wee Folk, had convinced him that the "Móra" were about as popular among Lily's people as the Wee Folk were in his village.

The afternoon passed as the morning had. Endymion knew that Lily was all right. He almost felt that he could see her—surrounded by her fellow villagers—in the square he'd glimpsed the day before through bleary, exhausted eyes.

But he couldn't.

At times, he got angry. Angry at Lily's mother. Angry at the Wee Folk. Angry at whoever had wiped the blazes from the trees. Angry at himself for knowing he'd never find Lily's village if he wandered off into the mountains without a trail.

Never angry at Lily. He couldn't be. He wouldn't.

Never.

SOUL-THREAD

L ily didn't make an appearance the next day, either. Endymion went through the motions. The sheep flocked around him on the trek back to the village in the evening, sensing his unhappiness. Urania wouldn't stop bleating.

Helen noticed that something was wrong with her son as they sat at the table that evening. He was hardly touching his food, and his laconic grunting in response to questions reminded her of his father—one nonverbal family member was enough.

"Endymion," she said trying to lighten the mood, "what's gotten into you? Did one of the sheep get tired of you and give you a taste of their woolly wrath?"

Endymion seemed not to notice his mother's joke. He grunted, picked up his spoon, and took a desultory bite from his bowl.

Try as she might, Helen wasn't able to get Endymion to open up.

* * *

When Endymion clambered down from his rocky perch the following noon, after a morning spent trying to spin his sling but mostly just holding it in his hands, a thrill shot through him. The familiar sight of a female shape clad in a Wee Folk cloak was standing beside the stream. Endymion's heart surged. He clasped a hand to his chest to quell the rush of hope. Then he realized—it wasn't Lily. She was too small, and she moved differently. She threw back her hood, revealing a face he'd never seen before.

"Móra," said the young woman calmly in greeting.

Endymion looked at her. While he'd never seen her face before, he still knew it. He'd studied Lily's features like he was learning a puzzle and seen Lily's mother's face in the village. He had heard Lily describe this face as prettier than her own. He shook his head in denial.

"Blossom," he said, inclining his head toward her.

For a moment, there was a bit of doubt in the Wee Folk woman's eyes. Endymion felt like he'd won a point. A point in a game neither of them was playing, perhaps, but a point nonetheless.

"Móra," she repeated, "My family, my village, my people, wish to thank you for what you did for Lily." Her expression was unreadable. "She is resting at home, but without your intervention..." She stopped as if she couldn't bring herself to say what would have happened.

Endymion searched her face. He could see how someone might say she was prettier than Lily—she was smaller, more delicate. More elfin. But the green eyes, red hair, and familiar traces of Lily in her features only made him miss Lily more.

"But," she continued, and Endymion felt as if a stone anchor were about to be cast into the pool of his heart, "You will not see Lily again." Blossom gave a dismissive shake of her head. "Lily has been told this as well, and she understands."

Endymion stood in shocked silence. He wasn't surprised, but he was left without a way to go on.

"Don't try to make your way through the mountains. Don't try to look for her."

"Or, what?" said Endymion.

"Or ...," Blossom's face grew grim. After a taut pause, she continued, "There's no place in this world for whatever was going on between the two of you. There's no place in this world for that sort of thing."

Then she turned and left him standing in the meadow, with only the sheep for company.

Endymion was running. He was running with Lily. They scrambled through the underbrush, fleeing Thudwhack—branches and tough leaves cutting their skin and holding them back as if the tangled greenery had tiny grasping hands.

Endymion snapped awake with a start. He was surprised to find himself in his own loft. He wasn't surprised to be drenched with sweat. He sat up, his heart still pounding, half-expecting the clawed branches to still clutch at him. He shook his head. It had only been a dream.

As the remnants of the dream faded, Endymion thought back to what Blossom had said. There was no way. There was no way that Lily was all right with their being separated. Endymion knew that Lily was missing him. He knew it in the same way he knew that he was still breathing. Each breath made her absence more painful, pulling her more deeply into his thoughts.

Endymion sighed and climbed out of bed. There was nothing for it. He was going to have to break his fast, take the sheep up the mountain, and go about his day—even though Lily wouldn't be there when the sun reached its highest point.

* * *

Calliope bleated her dawn command, telling Endymion and the rest of the flock that she was on watch as she led them onward through the fog.

The fog was thick this morning, a blanket of uncertainty, both gray and white at once. White when he looked an inch ahead; gray when he tried to see beyond.

Endymion thought they were getting close to the meadow. He couldn't tell by any kind of landmark, as they were buried in the clammy wool layer enveloping the mountains. But judging by the time they had been walking, it couldn't be too far.

There was a glimpse of red. A spot of brightness cut its way through the pale shroud of white. Endymion's heart leapt. Was Lily coming to him after all?

It was a flower—a fire lily, its vibrant crimson glowing through the mist. Endymion remembered a spot near the path where a small brush fire had burned last year. His mother had already taken all the blossoms she was going to from this patch, leaving the rest to bloom and go to seed.

Endymion steeled himself for another heart-lorn day without Lily.

Helen looked at Endymion. There was something in the corner of her eye—something devious. Endymion didn't like it. "Someone's joining us for evening supper," she said. Endymion glared at her, then sighed and asked the question she was fishing for.

"Who?" Skepticism edged his voice.

"Lena," Helen answered. "She's been telling her mother how she never sees you anymore—with you taking the sheep to the upper pasture every day." She nodded thoughtfully, the picture of compassionate concern.

* * *

Lena was a tall young woman, just a sliver shorter than Endymion. Her hair was a light enough brown that, in some places, they might have called it blonde—though there were no straw tops in Woolfold in the Dell.

"So, Endymion," she said gamely, as they sat around the evening table, wooden bowls of stew steaming in front of them, "where've you been?" She smiled gently at him. "I was starting to think you'd moved to Capitol."

Endymion gazed idly at a particular chunk of turnip floating on the surface of his stew. He poked it with his wooden spoon, trying to make it sink. The aroma of leeks and garlic rose from the bowl, reminding him how much he usually liked his mother's cooking.

Today, he felt muddy, muddled, and tired. He'd spent the day with the sheep in the mountains—and a day without Lily didn't feel like a day at all.

"Endymion," said Helen, her voice strained like wool pulled tight on a carding comb, "Lena asked you a question."

Endymion had always liked Lena. As children, they had

played together, running with the village offspring of a similar age. There had even been times he'd thought of her in *that* way.

Leaving behind the mystery of whether the nugget of turnip would float or sink, Endymion lifted his head. He tried—bravely—to fix his gaze on Lena. To see *her,* not some obstacle on the path back to Lily. But the flames dancing in the hearth, the dyed tapestry on the wall, even a red ribbon in Lena's hair—all of it conjured Lily's face in his mind, when he was supposed to be seeing Lena.

Endymion took ill. He struggled through the next day, but when he returned to the croft after putting the sheep into the fold in the evening, he collapsed. Helen got him into his bed and managed to spoon-feed him some broth, but when he woke in the morning with a fever, she sent Ewan to take care of the sheep and went to fetch Marj.

* * *

After Marj had examined Endymion, paying particular attention to his tongue for some reason, she straightened and turned to Helen with a thoughtful look. Endymion had fallen into a fitful, uneasy slumber.

"Now Helen," Marj said, adjusting her shawl, "You know me."

"I do," said Helen, frowning, as it sounded like Marj was about to start a conversation—and she wanted to hear what was wrong with her son.

"You know that I am not a superstitious woman," Marj went on.

Helen nodded.

"I believe in the modern study of magic. The rigorous, carefully defined spell crafting and potion making that we Cunning Folk, and the mages of the Academy, practice."

She hesitated. Then muttered, "Purple spots on his tongue."

Helen sighed, though under her breath so as not to offend Marjoram.

"I am familiar with many ailments and have a good idea of how to heal most of them," Marj continued.

"Please, Marj," said Helen, putting her hand on the cunning woman's arm.

"Of course," said Marj sympathetically. "I'll do what I can for him. I'll make a brew of willow bark and lavender. I'll prepare a heated poultice of garlic and honey. I'll give him a potion of Winterveil to try to reduce the fever, but ...,"

"But, what?" asked Helen.

"If I didn't know better," said Marj. "If I didn't know that the Wee Folk are not so different from us—and that believing otherwise is superstition—I'd think that your son had eaten of the fairy fruit."

Helen didn't know who started it or how it spread. Still, somehow, the rumor traveled through Woolfold— that Endymion had eaten something he shouldn't have. When Helen delivered an order of carded, spun yarn—dyed a fanciful green with woad and onion skins—to Mrs Silbern, she caught sight of Mr. Colwyk, the blacksmith. He turned his head and spat on the ground, a ward against the fae. On her way back through the village square, a group of older women, huddled in whispered conversation, fell silent as she passed. Even Ewan, whose social sensibilities resembled those of Urania, noticed the change in the village's mood.

* * *

There was a knock at the door. Endymion was up in his loft, sleeping off his fever. Ewan had taken the sheep up to the high pasture. Helen sighed, set down her wool carders, and got up to see who was there.

Tilda Pratt, the village's primary gossip spinner, rarely had reason to visit Helen. Known to everyone but herself as "Cawing Tilda," she was like a raven, swooping in to scavenge on the unfortunate.

"Good day, Tilda," Helen said with a nod to the sour-faced, plainly dressed woman standing in the doorway. "Won't you come in?"

"Don't mind if I do," Tilda said primly, pushing past Helen to move into the room. She attempted a smile as she entered— *attempted* being the operative word. It didn't entirely take. The effort looked as if the edges of her mouth had been hoisted upward with a block and tackle, only for the rope to snap.

"I'll brew us some mint," said Helen with another sigh.

"Is he up in the loft?" asked Tilda in a mock whisper as

Helen set the kettle near the coals to heat. The whisper was no quieter than her regular speaking voice, so Helen assumed she meant for Endymion to hear it.

"If, by he, you mean my son, Endymion, then yes," answered Helen, her features settling into a frown that Tilda didn't seem to notice.

"Elber Wain saw him," said Tilda, some kind of satisfaction showing on her face. "He was talking to one of them, he was." She leaned back, and breathed deeply, the catching of her breath in her throat making a sound like a pile of small sticks rattling when kicked. "A little one, a Fae. One of the Wee Folk. The whole village is talking about it. He's eaten something he shouldn't, hasn't he?"

"Tilda Pratt!" said Helen.

"There's talk he should be exiled," said Tilda, her features getting sterner, if that was possible, "Though some are opposing it, there are those that say that there's no place for any who eat of the fairy fruit in Woolfold in the Dell."

Helen's face hardened into stone. "Tilda Pratt," she said, her voice as cold as ice, "You will leave my house." She pointed at the door. "I never want to see you here again."

After Tilda left, Helen stood shaking at the door, heart pounding. She had made an enemy—perhaps more than one—but she would protect her son, whatever the village thought.

Endymion drifted in and out of consciousness. Each time he woke, his thoughts were of Lily. The fever, which Marj's Winterveil potion had lessened but not completely eliminated, still burned within him. The warmth in his body blended with vivid images of Lily's hair and the heat of their last kiss. He was on fire, for her.

He tossed and turned, thinking of her and sometimes of how sorry he felt for himself until he faded off into fitful slumber again.

Then, one time, when he awoke, something other than thoughts of Lily's flaming hair occupied his attention. Something had woken him. Something different than the heat of his fevered brow. The moonlight and traces of cool nighttime air squeezed their ways in through the cracks in the shuttered window.

There had been a tapping sound. It had blended with his dream. In the dream, it had been someone knocking at a door—though there was no door in his loft, just a shuttered window and the ladder leading down into the rest of the house.

Another tap echoed against the window. This time he was sure it was real. Something was rapping outside.

Endymion pulled the poultice, now cold, off his chest. It reeked of garlic and left a sticky mess behind it. He pulled on his clothes and staggered toward the window. Another tap echoed against the wood as he reached it.

He opened the shutter. Outside, a cloaked female figure stood on the ground below. In one hand, she held a small stone; in the other, a lamp that glittered with silvery light. Endymion's heart leapt again—*could it be Lily?* Then, by how she moved, he recognized Blossom.

Seeing him, Blossom dropped the stone, and motioned for him to come down.

Endymion worked his way over to the ladder, climbing down slowly and with great effort. Between his feverish weakness and the need to be quiet so as not to wake his parents, the descent felt like one of the hardest things he'd ever done.

He swayed over to the front door and lurched out into the night.

Blossom was waiting for him. She held up her silvery lantern, and in its glow he saw her face. A surge of longing for Lily's face, so similar and yet so different, washed over him. "Móra," she greeted him, her tone somewhat grim. She looked him over, noting his pallor in the lantern light, and the stiffness in his movements. "You look like you wrestled a plague-ridden ram—and lost."

Endymion tried to match her sternness. "Blossom," he replied. But, the thought that she might be here on Lily's behest filled him. "Where is she?" he asked. "Is she here?"

"No she's not here," said Blossom. "But, I'm here to take you to her—if you're able," she eyed him skeptically.

Endymion felt confused. "You said I'd never see her again."

"I did," said Blossom. Her expression softened a bit. "But things have changed."

"What's changed?" asked Endymion. As he looked at Blossom, he saw more and more of Lily's face in hers. Even in the chill night air, his cheeks started to feel warm.

"Lily's not feeling well," Blossom said. "In fact, she looks a little like you do."

"Lily," said Endymion. The warmth in his cheeks spread through his whole face. He reached down, and made a motion toward Blossom, like he was going to stoke her hair.

Blossom drew back. "There's something wrong with you, Móra," she said, but the softness in her tone belied the hardness in her words. "Can you walk? Well enough to travel to our village?"

"Sorry," said Endymion. Then the weight of her words sank in—he could see Lily again. "I'd crawl if I had to."

He knew it was foolish. He knew he might not make it. But the idea of never seeing her again—never knowing why—was worse than any fever.

Blossom almost smiled. "Let's hope it doesn't come to that." She turned toward the mountains. "This way."

Endymion started to follow, then staggered, almost fell, and put his hand down on Blossom's shoulder. She was surprisingly strong for her size, and was able to support him enough to keep him from landing on the ground.

"I can't carry you, Móra," she said.

Endymion shook himself, trying to clear his head in the cool night mountain air. "I can walk," he said, and strode on, forcing strength into his steps—though they wavered beneath the effort.

B lossom led the way. Endymion wondered how she knew the paths from his village into the mountains— seemingly as well as he did, if not better—but he didn't have the energy to dwell on it. All of his strength and focus were needed just to keep moving, placing one foot in front of the other along the narrow trails.

He felt hot and feverish, yet cold in the icy night air. Beads of sweat formed on his flushed brow, then, chilled by the mountain breeze, slipped down his face like frosty tears. He stumbled as he trudged along, feeling a bit like a toddler learning to use his legs for the first time.

Blossom looked back at him, concern on her face. Endymion wasn't sure if it was worry for his well being, or just frustration at how much he was slowing them down.

They followed the villager's trails toward the heights, until they reached a point as high in the mountains as Endymion's meadow. Then Blossom veered from the familiar paths, along a route he no longer knew. Even by the light of Blossom's lamp, Endymion could no longer see a trail, though the way was wide enough and easy to travel. Endymion looked for the circular blazes that Lily had shown him, but he couldn't find them. Either Blossom was forging a new path—or this trail was marked in a different way.

Endymion stumbled again. This time he fell to his knees and stayed there, unable to rise. Blossom turned back to help him.

"Móra," she said softly. "I'm sorry to do this to you." She shook her head, a flash of frustration crossing her face—as if she were upset with herself. "My mother says she'll be able to help you." She held out her hand to him. "She says it'll help Lily as well." When Endymion took her hand, she helped him up—surprisingly strong for someone her size.

The rest of the journey faded into a haze. The flicker of Blossom's lamp, the twisted shadows of the gnarled mountain trees and brush, the steady ache of each step—all faded together into a morass of sweat, chill, and exhaustion.

Somehow, despite their height disparity, Blossom managed to support Endymion, keeping him moving even when his legs had all but given out.

Finally, with a sigh of relief, Blossom guided them out of the brush and into a clearing near a wooden palisade wall. By the silvery glimmer of Blossom's lantern, Endymion recognized the flower-covered wall of the Wee Folk village—the one he had seen on the last day he'd seen Lily, though the gate was nowhere in sight.

"We're almost there," said Blossom with relief. She led him forward, moved some vines aside to reveal a carefully concealed doorway, and Endymion stumbled into the domain of the Wee Folk.

On the other side of the wall, Blossom extinguished her lantern. As the light from the lamp faded, it was replaced by another silvery glow. At first, Endymion wasn't sure where the light was coming from—then he saw that the glittering cobblestones he had seen when he was last here were gleaming as if infused with the radiance of the moon. It was a subtle light, but the space was as bright as a full-moon night.

There was a thin layer of greenery along the wall, between the flower-coated wood of the palisade and the edge of the cobbles. Blossom led Endymion along the grass, trying to keep a veil of foliage between them and any late-night wanderers.

"Are we hiding?" asked Endymion.

"Shhh," said Blossom.

As they moved quietly between the wall and the foliage, Endymion looked at what he could see of the village. His exhaustion made it hard to focus, but this was his one chance to glimpse how the Wee Folk lived—and even through his fog of fatigue, curiosity stirred in him.

As before, he noticed two distinct kinds of houses. Some were built of stone, partly tucked into the rough rock cliffs lining the cobbled paths and byways. Others seemed to grow from the trunks of large trees, their doorways and windows not cut into the bark but rather shaped, as if the trees had chosen to open themselves. Endymion didn't recognize the trees. They were a kind he had never seen before—and certainly larger than any others that grew in the mountains.

Most of the windows in the houses were dark, though a few showed glimmering lights—signs, perhaps, of someone burning the midnight oil or whatever passed for oil in the lanterns of the Wee Folk. Blossom led him to a house near the palisade wall that didn't show any trace of light. It was one of the tree-trunk dwellings. Even Endymion, unfamiliar as he was with this village, could tell that this house wasn't occupied. It looked forlorn, somehow, as if the tree were pining for warmth and love.

Blossom brought him to the door—which swung smoothly open as they approached—and quickly ushered him inside. By the dim glow of another lamp within, Endymion saw the woman he had assumed was Lily's mother waiting.

"Finally," she said and closed the door behind them with a swift, quiet motion.

ndymion gazed at the woman he believed was the mother of his Lily. Something about her demanded respect, though her stature was as modest as Blossom's. Both of them would look small, standing next to Lily.

"Ma'am," he said carefully, trying to nod his head graciously. The effort brought a rush of blood to his fevered brow, and without Blossom rushing to support him, he would have fallen.

"You look like the leavings of a constipated tree squirrel, but you're still standing, so that's something." She pointed for Blossom to help him to a cot against one wall. "And, you can call me Sorrel." Sorrel exchanged a brief look with Blossom as she helped Endymion settle. He couldn't read the expression.

He scanned the room in the glow of Sorrel's one lantern. The floor and walls were made of wood—he could clearly see the grain winding through the material—but it wasn't cut or nailed. It seemed as if the whole room, from floor to ceiling, had been grown from the living heart of the tree.

"Where's Lily," he murmured, turning to Blossom. "You said she'd be here."

"I thought... maybe...," said Blossom, her voice uncertain. She glanced at her mother. Sorrel shook her head.

Then Sorrel shifted her gaze to Endymion. "Lie back," she said, pressing firmly but not unkindly against his chest.

Endymion obeyed. The cot held a soft blanket and a pillow at one end. It was surprisingly comfortable.

"I want to see Lily," he said blearily.

"Open your mouth," Sorrel replied. She poked and prodded at him for a few minutes. It reminded him of Marj's examination from a few days ago. The warmth in the heart of the tree and the soft lighting made him relax. Even Sorrel's prodding made him feel cared for. She was firm yet gentle in her own way. She inspected his tongue as Marj had.

If it hadn't been for his thoughts of Lily, Endymion might have drifted off to a fevered sleep. As it was, he tried again.

"Lily?" he asked.

"Can you help him?" Blossom asked her mother.

Sorrel nodded and turned to Endymion. "You're going to be fine," she said, "but there's something you need to know first."

Endymion looked at Sorrel. He tried to read her eyes, but her feelings were too complex—made up of too many emotions. There was sorrow in there. There was pity. Compassion made an appearance, though it was hiding behind a veil of pride. He thought he saw some traces of empathy, but somehow, anger made its way into the picture and shoved the empathy to one side.

"You and my daughter have soul-threaded," Sorrel said. "I'd call both, or either one of you, stupid, but I know that soul-threading is an involuntary interaction, and you don't have any control over it."

"What does that mean?" Endymion asked, his voice quavering a little though he tried to keep it firm.

Sorrel frowned. "It's not something I ever thought I would be explaining to a Móra," she said, "Let alone one who was soul-threaded with my daughter."

"I want to see her," said Endymion listlessly, looking at the wall as if he was looking through it.

"Of course you do," said Sorrel. Her voice changed. She sounded like a teacher addressing a classroom. "Soul-threading is when two souls form a bond. It's not a requirement among the Wee Folk for joining, but it adds weight to the union." Her gaze softened in sympathy. "The two souls become tied together, as if with an invisible thread. There are some advantages, but more obstacles. Your illness is one of the latter. Among the Wee Folk, it's said that soul-threading leaves one always knowing where your bondmate is."

She reached out—and somehow, a pair of shears was already in her hand. She snipped a lock of hair off of his head.

Endymion clapped his hand to his scalp. He had the

impulse to say, "Ow," but, of course, it hadn't hurt.

"What does that mean?" he repeated.

Sorrel brought something out from behind her. Perhaps it came from one of the multitude of tiny pouches on her belt; possibly she summoned it from the air. It was a lanyard strung with an amber amulet, glowing softly like captured sunlight.

"Touch this," she said.

Endymion reached out and laid a fingertip against the honey-hued gem. Almost at once, a flicker of relief stirred in him —Not full wellness, but improvement. His brow cooled, and he felt a little stronger.

Endymion sat up and studied the amulet, shimmering like an afternoon sunset. He saw something inside the hardened resin. It was a lock of hair similar to the one that Sorrel had just snipped off his head. The hair's color was lost in the amber's molten glow.

Before Endymion could ask, Sorrel answered his unspoken question. "It's Lily's," she said. Her eyes searched his as though peering into the depths of his soul. "Contact with a part of the one you're soul-threaded to can ease the Separation Sorrow." She paused, thoughtful. "Hair is one of the simplest solutions."

"I don't need this if I can see Lily," Endymion said as Sorrel slipped the amulet over his head. The touch of the amber stone on his chest was cool and soothing.

Sorrel didn't reply. She resumed her poking and prodding, presumably to gauge the amulet's effect.

"Back in my village, they thought I'd eaten of the fairy fruit."

Sorrel laughed. She had a pleasant laugh. It reminded Endymion of her daughter's.

"I wish it were so simple," she said. "I have two challenges ahead of me—near-hopeless tasks. First, I need to solve the cruel riddle of how my daughter came to be soul-threaded to a Móra." She shook her head, her voice tight with emotion. "And second, I must learn how to cut a thread that no one has ever severed before."

She met Endymion's eyes.

"Breaking a dependence on some *fruit* would be as easy as catching moonlight in a mirror, by contrast."

"Cut a thread?" asked Endymion, a chill of realization stealing over him. "Cut?" he repeated. "I don't want anything cut."

He stirred, trying to rise from the cot. Sorrel placed a hand firmly on his chest, and again, he was startled by her strength.

"Easy, Móra," said Sorrel. "Blossom?" she called out.

"I want to see Lily," Endymion said, beginning to struggle against her grip.

Blossom joined her mother, working to hold him down.

"Lily!" Endymion called out.

There was a flash of panic in Sorrel's eyes. Suddenly and surely he sensed she had a reason to keep his presence secret. He opened his mouth to call again.

But as quickly as before, Sorrel drew a small herb pot from her belt and thrust it beneath Endymion's nose. The now-familiar, cloying scent from the pot overtook him before he could resist. The world spun and faded to black.

FAIRY FRUIT

E ndymion woke in his own bed. He might have taken the whole thing for a fever dream—until his fingers touched the cool smoothness of the amber gemstone that hung on its lanyard around his neck.

He felt better. In fact, he felt better than he had in a week. He hadn't been outside in days. Long enough, he supposed, for people to talk about him.

Endymion jumped out of bed. A plan began to form in his mind. He would take the sheep up to the meadow, then leave them. Calliope could handle the flock for a few hours. Then —missing trails be damned—he would find his way to Lily's village, and confront Sorrel. Nothing would keep him and Lily apart.

He paused.

What if Lily didn't want to see him? What if she had known that he was in the village, and hadn't come on purpose?

What if Sorrel cutting whatever thread bound them was really for the best?

Endymion dismissed the thought with a shake of his head.

He knew Lily missed him—just as much as he missed her. He knew it as surely as he knew his heart was still beating.

His fingers returned to the amulet. Somehow, Lily's presence seeped from it and calmed him. She felt near—even though she was far away.

He dressed, then climbed down the ladder. His legs felt stronger on the rungs than they had in days.

Helen looked up, startled. A web of fibers stretched between her wool carders.

"Endymion," she said, "you're up!"

"I'm feeling much better, Mama," said Endymion. "I'm ready to take the sheep up to the high pasture."

Helen frowned. "Not today, Endymion," she said. "Your father's already taken them." Her frown deepened. "And, anyway, I don't think you should leave the house today. The talk in the town has taken a dangerous turn."

There was an urgent knock at the door. "Who could that be?" asked Helen, rising from her seat at the main table. The table was multipurpose: their dining table, Ewan's carving bench of an evening, and the platform where, come spring, they sheared the sheep.

This morning, it served a more ordinary role: Helen's workbench for carding tangled, rough wool—the first step in turning it into yarn.

Helen frowned as she crossed to the door. It was unusual to have someone knock this early.

When she opened the door, Leland burst in, panting like he'd outrun a wolf pack.

"Leland," Helen chided, her voice edged with motherly reproach at the suddenness of his entrance.

"Endymion," Leland gasped, "you've got to leave. You've got to get out." He glanced around wildly looking for a back door, though he knew—as well as they did—that the cottage had only one entrance.

"They're coming."

"Who's coming, Leland?" said Helen.

"My father," panted Leland. "My father," he repeated, "with the blacksmith. And Mrs. Pratt."

Endymion shook his head. He couldn't guess why Leland's father would be coming over this early in the morning—let alone the blacksmith, or Mrs. Pratt.

Helen, on the other hand, seemed to have some idea. A flash of panic showed on her face—quickly replaced by her habitual expression of competent calm.

"Endymion," she said. "Climb upstairs and grab your pocket. And a few things that might be useful on a trip. I'll get you some food."

Leland looked skeptical, his glance flickering toward the door. "They weren't that far behind me."

Helen nodded. "Hurry," she said to Endymion.

Endymion clambered up the ladder, his lifelong habit of obeying his mother quieting the questions tumbling through his mind.

He picked up his pocket and glanced around the loft. Did he have time to grab his cloak? Should he put on his work boots?

The sounds of Helen packing food below reached him. Then came a thunderous pounding at the door.

H elen stepped toward it—whether to open it or drop the bar to hold it shut wasn't clear. In the end, it didn't matter. The door crashed open before she could do either. A powerful-looking man, Mr. Colwyk, the town blacksmith, shouldered his way through the entryway. He held the door open for the two people trailing behind him.

"What's the meaning of this?" demanded Helen indignantly. "What are you doing, bursting into my home without permission?"

The first of the two people who followed Mr. Colwyk stepped forward: Leland's father. He swept the room with an imperious gaze. His eye fell on his son, trying—and failing—to be invisible in one corner. He frowned.

Godric Branhelm was the First Voice of the Moot. When the village council gathered to discuss town matters, he led —and often dominated—the sessions. That position granted him a certain authority outside of those meetings, which he used freely—and abused just as often. He had dressed for the occasion, it seemed, in his best going-to-church clothes: a stiff black suit with a starched collar that must have pressed into his neck. His gray hair hung to just above that collar.

Tilda Pratt, the third invader, sidled into the room close on the heels of the Moot's Voice. She took up a perch behind his right shoulder, where she could observe—near enough to see it all, but distant enough to claim she'd only been watching.

"The meaning of this," said Mr. Branhelm, "is that we're looking for your son." He lifted his nose into the air while glaring over the length of it at Helen. "We're here to detain him for suspicion of Fae contamination, by order of the Moot."

Mrs. Pratt sniffed wisely, as if to let everyone see she'd

known it all along.

"Very brave, Godric," said Helen. "Waiting until you knew that Ewan was gone, and bringing your pet smith." She nodded to the burly man, whose face was only beginning to register her comment. "Ethelred," she said. He blinked, his brow furrowing, as though weighing her words. A moment later, his jaw tightened as the meaning settled in.

Godric Branhelm had the decency to flush at Helen's comment, but it only seemed to harden his resolve.

"Is the boy here?" he asked.

Endymion didn't wait to be summoned. He slipped a hand beneath his tunic, rubbed the smooth surface of the locket with Lily's hair—for luck—and started down the ladder.

E veryone froze in a tense tableau. Tilda tittered—a nervous sound that made her seem even more birdlike. Leland twitched as if he meant to rise. The smith reacted first to Endymion's presence—he started to move forward.

"Stop right where you are, Ethelred," said Helen. "I won't have you treating my boy like a criminal."

The burly man stopped as if he'd struck a wall, then looked to Mr. Branhelm with a bewildered expression.

"You're looking for me, sir?" asked Endymion, his gaze trailing up Mr. Branhelm's stiff, starched collar on the way to his face.

"Godric," said Helen, "if you must do this, at least let us do it in a civilized manner." She shook her head and gestured toward the food she had been preparing. "Why don't you and your tame ox"—she turned to the smith and, with a loving smile, added—"no offense, Ethelred." Turning back to Mr. Branhelm, she continued, "Leave us until we've broken our morning fast." Her voice firmed as she spoke. "We'll be glad to come by later and talk to you about whatever silliness you and the Moot think necessary."

Tilda gasped.

"I'm sorry, Helen," said Mr. Branhelm, the undertone of satisfaction in his voice belying his words, "but I'm afraid we can't do that. The charges are serious." He frowned. "It was before your time in the village, but everyone here remembers the Red Spring." For a moment, he seemed almost human. "My son died that year."

His voice caught briefly, but he pushed on as if the memory were a cold wind to be shut out. He shook his head and continued. "We cannot allow even a trace of Fairy Fruit contamination to enter this village. Who knows what kind of depravity and immoral behavior that might lead to." He nodded to the blacksmith. "Mr. Colwyk, you will take the boy into custody."

The blacksmith placed a meaty hand on Endymion's shoulder. It felt like a vise.

"What's that he's got around his neck?" squawked Tilda.

Endymion clutched one hand protectively over the amulet beneath his linen tunic. He felt the comforting sense of Lily's presence both where the amulet touched his skin, and through the cloth beneath his palm.

The blacksmith, still holding Endymion's shoulder in a vice-like grip, reached with his other hand to pull the chain around the boy's neck, spilling the medallion into the sunlight streaming through the window. The amber stone glowed fiercely in the morning light.

Tilda gasped again. At this point, you'd think that was her only purpose in the group.

Helen looked—for just a second—as surprised as any of the three invaders. But the expression vanished before anyone could notice.

"It's worse than I thought," said Mr. Branhelm triumphantly, "They've already been giving him gifts."

"Don't be silly," said Helen calmly. "I gave that to him." She stepped over to Endymion, and touched the honey-gold gem lovingly. "It's an old family heirloom." Her voice softened. "My mother gave it to me, and I passed it on to my son."

Something in Mr. Branhelm's face fell, as if he'd lost a grip on a weapon he'd been hoping to use. He watched as Endymion tucked the stone back under his tunic.

"Ethelred," he said shortly, "bring him." He turned to look at Tilda. "Tilda, bring the food. He can eat in the cell."

"Me?" cawed Tilda.

Mr. Branhelm just glared at her. She scuttled over to the table, giving Helen as wide a berth as possible.

"The Moot will meet to talk about this?" asked Helen angrily.

"Of course," said Godric, trying to sound reasonable now that he'd gotten his way. "The Moot will meet on Woden's Day."

"You're going to keep him locked up until then?" Storm clouds gathered behind Helen's eyes.

"Locked up and isolated," said Godric. "We don't know how bad the contamination has gotten."

W oolfold in the Dell didn't have a jail. In fact, it didn't have a cell for holding prisoners—not one constructed for the purpose, or even one originally built for something else. Mr. Branhelm had instructed the family servant (the Branhelms were rich enough to have a servant—and more than one root cellar) to clear out the kitchen root cellar. The servant's name was Ellie, and she had once been a classmate of Endymion, Leland, and Lana.

Mr. Branhelm's style of governance—he had been the First Voice of the Moot for quite some time—might have lent itself to having a jail, or at least a single prison cell tucked away somewhere. But he didn't actually have as much power as he would have liked. The office of First Voice simply meant his was the first voice—and perhaps the loudest—at the moots.

Ellie had arranged the emptied root cellar with a clean straw pallet in one corner, and Mr. Colwyk unceremoniously left Endymion there. Tilda Pratt scrabbled across the room to leave the food that she'd taken from Helen's table on the pallet, then fluttered away, clearly flustered by how involved she'd become. She practically flew up the narrow stone stair that led to the Branhelms' kitchen.

When Mr. Colwyk left, slamming the solid wooden trapdoor at the top of the stair behind him, Endymion was left alone in the small mostly empty room—lit only by the flickering light of a single oil sconce.

The walls were lined with shelves, mostly cleared out by Ellie. Some of the heavier stores had been left behind: boxes of root vegetables, sacks of meal, and a few slabs of salted mutton. The room smelled strongly of food, and it reminded Endymion that he hadn't yet broken his fast. He glanced at the bundle Tilda had left and hoped she'd been flustered enough not to notice that it was more like a traveler's meal than a morning one.

It was cold in the cellar, and Endymion pulled his cloak a little tighter around himself as he sat cross-legged on the straw pallet to eat. He reached under his tunic and rubbed the smooth surface of the amber amulet with Lily's hair in it. He thought he felt a little warmth flow into his finger from the stone.

The water pot for the tea was hissing softly on the fire. A wisp of steam crept out from where the lid didn't quite meet the rim. Helen gazed at it impatiently. She hadn't come here to drink tea—not even Marj's chamomile infusion, which she usually liked.

Marj was sitting in her regular chair, leaning back a little. The chair creaked in protest. There was a reason why the neighborhood children—when they were behaving badly—called her "large Marj."

"I didn't come here to drink tea, Marj," said Helen, voicing her thoughts aloud.

"Be a dear and take the pot off the fire," said Marj. She let the chair return to its usual position, all four feet on the ground. It groaned in relief.

While Helen poured the tea into wooden cups, Marj got to the point.

"I know it's hard to do nothing, Helen," she said. "But for now, it's probably best." She frowned. "Godric Branhelm is a puffed-up rooster. And, I hate the superstitious beliefs that led the Moot to vote for Endymion's arrest. Still, if we present the case on Woden's day, and if the fearful fools see that nothing magical has happened while he's being held, then we can almost certainly convince them that the dangers of the 'fairy fruit' are imagined."

"I can't just do nothing, Marj," said Helen, her voice coming close to cracking on the word *nothing*. "They've shut my son away."

"Maybe you should go to see him," said Marj. "I'm sure Godric will let you talk to him, especially if I ask." She touched one finger thoughtfully to her chin. "As you know, we cunning folk have a rule to stay out of the local government's business, in exchange for them staying out of ours, but I still have pull with them." She shook her head. "After all, I helped Godric's wife when their son was born." Her face lengthened a little with grief. "Such a tragedy, that was."

"The Red Spring," said Helen. "I've heard a little about what happened that season." She met Marj's gaze firmly. "You were there." A pause. "Can you tell me more?"

Marj leaned back in her chair again and took a sip from her steaming wooden cup. "It was a long time ago," she said. "Godric's son, Oswin, was about sixteen, or so." She hesitated, as if unsure whether what she was about to say might bother Helen, "Not unlike your Endymion."

Helen leaned forward, trying to absorb every word, as if Endymion's fate might rest solely on her understanding of Marj's story.

"His friend, Tomlin, was about the same age." She slowed a little, remembering. "You never saw them apart. They were inseparable—close as twins, though born to separate mothers." Marj took another sip from her cup. "They were good boys, somewhat surprisingly, considering Godric was the father of one. But even he was younger then. Different.

"Good boys," continued Marj, "but wild and restless. Always off exploring the hills. Even their parents—sometimes especially their parents—couldn't keep track of them.

"It wasn't just the boys," Marj noted. "It was a restless spring for everyone. Even I—just a young slip of a girl at thirty-eight, or thereabouts—felt it. There was something in the air. And the boys were of that age where you go looking for something you can't quite name."

Helen reserved judgment on whether someone nearing forty could still count as a "young slip of a girl."

Marj's expression grew grim. "It seems they found it. Godric was the first to notice. He complained to the Moot. He wasn't the Voice at that time, but they still listened to him. He told them something wasn't right with his son. He came home from the hills with flowers in his hair. Lilies, I think. Of course, Godric had no sympathy for anything like that."

She snorted in disbelief. "He hummed songs that Godric had never heard before—strange ones. Unnatural. 'Ungodly' was the word he used, I think."

Helen nodded. It wasn't the same, not exactly—but something about Marj's story reminded her of Endymion lately.

"Tomlin's parents had noticed strange things, too. They weren't as bothered by it as Godric was, but they'd seen changes—odd behaviors, odd words."

"Had they really eaten anything?" asked Helen.

Marj shook her head. "Something was going on," she said, "and I'll tell you what I think it was, but—" She paused, and wiped a trace of a tear from the corner of her eye, "but it wasn't those boys, or any kind of fairy fruit that turned that spring red. It was Godric and the Moot."

She lifted the steaming pot and poured more of the chamomile infusion into her mug. "Godric and the Moot started it—and in the end, they finished it too."

There was a knock on the trapdoor—quiet, almost tentative. Endymion hardly heard it at first. He had been resting on the pallet, since there wasn't much else to do. He sat up, listening, uncertain whether he'd actually heard a sound. A second knock followed—a little firmer this time.

Endymion rose and climbed up the short stone stair to just beneath the closed trapdoor.

"Endymion?" came a quiet voice through the thick wood.

Endymion wasn't sure whose voice it was at first. The sound was muffled, and it wasn't one of the voices he'd expected to hear. Then he remembered who worked as the servant in the Branhelm household.

"Ellie?" he said, speaking a little louder than he might have otherwise, so his voice would carry through the trapdoor. He remembered her from their school days—quieter than Lana, kind, and always willing to share her lunch when someone forgot theirs.

"Endymion," came Ellie's voice a little firmer this time. "I need to give you some lamp oil." There was a pause. "And I've made you some supper." She paused again. This one felt awkward to Endymion, almost like Ellie thought she was asking too much. "Could you please stand away from the door? Mr. Branhelm told us not to get too close to you." A last pause —Endymion had the sense she was working up to something. "And…" a brief silence, "could you please not try to come out? I don't have a way to stop you, but I'll get in a lot of trouble if you do."

Endymion took a moment before replying. "Of course, Ellie," he said gently. "I won't do anything to cause trouble for you."

He stepped back down to the bottom of the stair. He watched as the heavy trapdoor lifted into the air. He had been in Leland's house before and admired the clever pulley system— one even someone as slight as Ellie could operate.

As he watched Ellie place a small stoppered glass flask of oil on the top step beside a dinner tray, he considered how easily he could dash up the stairs, push her aside, and flee the house.

He shook his head. He couldn't do that to her, not after she'd asked him not to.

"I haven't filled the sconce in a while," said Ellie. "It's probably about time. There's a candle near the lamp. You'll need to light it first, so you can see to refill the sconce." Endymion thought he heard an unmistakable trace of warmth in her voice as she continued. "The supper is a lamb stew. I added extra carrots. I hope you like it."

The heavy wooden trapdoor crashed shut. Endymion heard the deadbolt click into place.

Marj continued, "There was a Wee Folk village not too terribly far away." She glanced up at Helen's face. "Still is, I believe." She lowered her eyes to the floor, as if turning her gaze from something painful. "It used to be called Greymoss Rest."

"Used to be?" asked Helen.

"If they haven't renamed it…" said Marj. "If they haven't moved away… A lot changed that spring."

"I knew it was there," said Helen quietly.

"We used to trade with them," Marj resumed. "We used to have a—limited to be sure—relationship with the Wee Folk." Marj, usually one of the most cheerful people Helen knew, sounded as grim as Helen had ever heard her. "I should have done more, but I was trying to stick to my principles. To not interfere."

"What happened?" asked Helen breathlessly.

"There was some kind of confrontation. Godric met with his son, Oswin, and they fought. Godric came back from the meeting yelling about the fairy fruit and how the Fae had stolen his son from him." She shook her head. "I think Tomlin met with his parents, too. They didn't fight in the same way, but it was the same feeling. That they'd lost their son."

Helen thought about what she was hearing. She'd picked up some of this from hints that people had dropped, but no one in the village, not even Ewan, ever openly talked about it.

"You know what I think happened?" asked Marj.

"I've my thoughts, but yours weigh heavier."

"I think they fell in love." She nodded, affirming her guess to herself. "I think they met two Wee Folk girls, and as any sixteen-year-old boys would, they fell in love." She glanced at Helen, and Helen noticed that the corners of her eyes were glistening with moisture. "They couldn't tell their parents, as falling in love with a Wee Folk girl is obviously even worse than becoming addicted to Fairy Fruit." She shook her head. "At that age, nothing feels more important than your first love."

Marj snorted again. "The fruit is just fruit," she said. "Sweet, maybe different than we grow here—but it wasn't what changed them." She looked wistful for a moment. "First love. That's what's magical."

Helen stared at the older woman, her throat suddenly dry. In her mind's eye, she saw Endymion's face as he'd looked when she'd last seen him—resolute, frightened, yet still full of some emotion she'd never seen in him before. Could he have found someone to love?

Helen stood and lifted the pot from the table. It was still warm, though not hot. "Some more?" she asked Marj. Without waiting for a response, she refilled both her own and Marj's cup with the mild brew. A faint mist rose from the warm fluid, and the sweet floral scent of chamomile wafted through the room.

"That's when things took a turn for the worse," said Marj. "Are you sure you want to hear this?"

"I have to," answered Helen. "I think knowing what happened back then might help me defend Endymion." Her eyes hardened. "And it may help me understand something about Godric."

A log in the fire split with a crack. The herbs hanging over the chimney rustled faintly, as if uneasy in the heat.

Marj's mouth thinned. "No one's ever going to understand him," she said. The cunning woman sighed and leaned toward Helen. The chair creaked again. "Godric tried to get the Moot to make all the men and boys join a militia. He wanted the whole village to take up arms and attack the Rest." She shook her head. "That was a failure. This is a village of shepherds and sheep. I don't think there's a sword in the whole town."

"Did the Wee Folk do anything?" asked Helen.

Marj frowned. "They should have." She peered down at her cup, as if the answers to the past were floating in a warm bath of chamomile. "Like I said, back then, there was still some trade. There was a clear pathway between Greymoss Rest and Woolfold in the Dell. After... After that spring, they closed it somehow. The path disappeared. More than that, people who've tried to find the Rest—and a few have—get lost." Marj pressed her lips together. "The Wee Folk have their own magic. It's nothing like the magic of the cunning folk—nor even what the wizards teach at the Academy."

Marj's jaw tightened. "They should have closed it before. They didn't know. I don't think they could have imagined what Godric was capable of."

For a moment, neither of them spoke. In the silence, a low creak rose briefly from the warm laid-work of the hearth, as if the weight of Marj's story was too much for the stones to bear.

Marj went on. "After Godric failed to get the folk of Woolfold to take up arms, he went another direction." She ran a hand through her hair. Helen, for the first time, wondered how that hair had looked when it was all brown, before the streaks of gray had come to grant Marj her quiet authority. "He didn't tell anyone he was doing this, at least not me or the general Moot council, but he wrote to the Baron."

"The Baron?" Helen's eyes narrowed.

"The Lord of the Western Marches," Marj shook her head. "To this day, I'm amazed and a little impressed that he had the audacity."

Helen's brow furrowed. Marj found herself wondering what Helen was thinking. Nobody knew where Helen had come from before she met Ewan and moved to Woolfold—she didn't talk about it—but rumor had it her status had been higher than anything seen in a little sheep-herding town. Marj didn't let the thought interrupt her story.

"I don't know what he wrote, but it must have been quite compelling," she continued. "The Baron sent a detachment of soldiers." Her lips tightened. "When they marched into town, it was like a harvest parade. Everyone lined up to see them." She frowned. "If we'd only known..."

"What happened?"

"Godric tried to talk to them," Marj said, sounding more somber with each word. "He tried to keep some sort of control over what they did." She rubbed her forehead as if the memory pained her. "The captain of the company was young. I think he was trying to impress his superiors. It might have been his first command." A log shifted in the hearth. "He didn't listen to a word Godric said. Some rustic, from a shepherding mud-hole, trying to tell an officer of the Baron's guard what to do." She dropped her gaze to the rushes on the floor. "He asked Godric where the Wee Folk village was, and they marched off down the path.

"To his credit—or perhaps his blame—I think Godric realized that he'd started something he shouldn't have. He got a few of the members of the Moot together, snatched up whatever could pass for a weapon, and followed the soldiers.

"We didn't know what had happened until they got back." Marj's expression clouded.

Helen resisted the urge to reach out and put her hand on the older woman's shoulder. She needed to hear how it ended.

"The soldiers just marched through town without stopping. They didn't tell anyone anything." Marj's eyes were watering again. Though it had happened long ago, telling it unearthed old feelings.

"We didn't learn the truth until Godric and the others returned."

Marj's voice shook as she went on. "Godric was carrying his son's body." She peered into the flames of the fire, searching for some kind of solace there. "Oswin was a good lad," she said. "I think he fought to defend the village against the soldiers." She paused, then continued. "I don't know what happened to Tomlin. No one ever saw him again.

"Godric told us, Marj said. "Though he could hardly speak..." Her voice broke a little. "He told us that it had been quick."

"Quick," repeated Helen, having no idea what to say.

"I think they—" Marj met Helen's eyes. "The Wee Folk. I don't think they had any weapons either." She glanced back at the floor. "Maybe hunting bows and some knives." Her voice turned grim. "I bet they do now."

"How many died?" asked Helen.

Marj shook her head. "It wasn't a slaughter. I think that the soldiers were largely trying to scare them. I think most of them ran away." She paused before continuing. "Godric said there were some other bodies. The soldiers set some fires. I don't know what that captain thought he was accomplishing. All he really did was make that village hate and fear us."

"Oswin?" Helen asked softly.

"I think..." Marj said. "I think he didn't really know what was going on. I think he tried to defend his new friends. I think he challenged the wrong soldier when he should have been hiding or running."

Helen stared at the cunning woman in silence. She'd heard hints over the years, but this was the first time anyone had ever told her what happened in the Red Spring without evasion.

"Godric got the wrong message from the whole thing, of

course," Marj said bitterly. "He couldn't blame himself, so he got even more obsessed with the fairy fruit, and started telling anyone who'd listen about how the Fae folk killed his son."

She nodded thoughtfully. "It's a lot easier, I suppose, than admitting the boy died because of what he did."

Helen shook her head slowly. "And now he's doing it again. Blaming the Fae. Blaming the fruit. Instead of seeing what's really in front of him."

LOST

Endymion heard a voice calling through the door. He had no difficulty recognizing this voice. He'd known it his whole life. "Mama," he called out, rushing to the staircase and climbing partway up.

"I'm sorry Endymion," said Helen's voice, muffled just a bit by the wood, "Godric won't let me open the door." She mumbled something under her breath, then repeated what might have been the same thing louder. "The man's got dags for brains. Thinks he's in charge of everything."

There was a small metal grill set into the trapdoor—maybe for ventilation. Endymion hadn't noticed it before. Helen slid back the little metal cover, and her voice came through more clearly.

"How are you doing, Endymion?" she asked, a note of maternal concern in her tone. "Have they been giving you enough to eat?"

"I'm fine," said Endymion, trying not to let his manner betray how false his words were. "Ellie's been cooking for me." He hesitated, then his breath caught as he asked, "When are they going to let me out of here?" He peered through the gloom, hoping to catch a glimpse of his mother's face through the small opening.

"I'm working on it," said Helen grimly. Then her voice changed as she asked, "Endymion?" A pause. "Where did that amulet come from?"

Endymion hesitated.

"Endymion?" Helen repeated.

"I met a girl," said Endymion slowly. "I really like her," the words poured out in a rush. "You'd really like her." Even faster. "Her hair's like the fire lily flower. She's beautiful." He paused.

"And," slower now. "She's really smart. She's as smart as you are. She knows so many things." Endymion stopped talking, as if realizing what he had said. He waited for her reaction.

There was a long silence, then Helen's voice dropped into it like a stone breaking the surface of still water deep in a well.

"So Godric wasn't entirely wrong," said Helen slowly. Her voice had gone cold. Endymion couldn't read it. Another pause. "And when you came home asking about the fruits in your lunch?"

"They taste really good," said Endymion. He shook his head, though there was no way Helen could see the gesture. "But, there's nothing wrong with them. They're just fruit." He thought for a moment, then said more softly, "And anyway, Lily would never give me anything that would be bad for me."

At first, Endymion wasn't sure what was going on. He'd been having a conversation with Calliope, who, it seemed, could speak quite well. They were discussing Calliope's feelings about Lily's proposal that, if she were the shepherdess, she would rename the sheep after the stars, rather than the muses.

Much to Endymion's satisfaction, Calliope didn't like the idea of being renamed. She expressed her contentment with her name, telling Endymion it suited her and she didn't want to part with it.

Endymion couldn't wait to tell Lily. He planned to rub her pert, perfect little nose in it a bit. She wasn't always right, after all.

Then Ellie showed up. This was the source of Endymion's confusion. What was Ellie doing in his meadow, interrupting a perfectly reasonable conversation with a sheep? And why was she telling him to wake up? And so insistently?

Endymion opened his eyes to the dank root cellar. Ellie was leaning over him. The lantern she held threw shadows that competed with the glow from the wall sconce. At first, he flinched—then, unexpectedly, he had the urge to hug her. She was the first person he'd seen in days.

"Endymion," she whispered urgently. "You've got to get up."

Endymion blinked. "What's going on?" he murmured groggily.

"I'm going to get you out," said Ellie. There was pride in her voice, but fear under it. "Leland says his father's out of control. He doesn't know what he'll do." She studied the stones at her feet. "The Moot is discussing banishment, or even execution."

Endymion shook his head, trying to clear the waking fog from his brain.

"Execution?" he repeated. A chill ran down his spine. "You're not serious."

"Leland says," she glanced away, as if that might soften Endymion's reaction to what she was saying. He noticed something soft in the way she said Leland's name. "That we don't have a choice—we have to get you out."

"Where am I to go?" he asked. "I don't have anything with me. I can't go home, they'd just find me again."

Ellie shook her head. Her voice trembled a bit as she said, "Leland's waiting for you outside. He brought some things for you."

Endymion let out a slow breath and pulled the blanket off his shoulders. "All right," he said. "Let's go."

A s they climbed the stairs and passed through the open trapdoor, Endymion noticed something on the edge of the wooden door, near the iron lock. A scattering of powder gleamed dimly in the light of Ellie's lantern. He leaned down for a closer look. Within the sparkling dust, the edges of the lock were singed, as if something had flared or burst near the metal. A faint, slightly uncanny herbal smell lingered in the air.

"What's this?" he asked, pointing at the lock.

Ellie held her finger to her lips, rolling her eyes upward to warn him not to wake the sleepers above. She squinted at the lock with an odd expression. "That was my idea," she whispered, a touch of pride threading through her quiet words. "They'll think the Fae broke you out. They won't suspect me."

Something about this bothered Endymion. Even through the fog of being woken in the middle of the night, he felt like something was wrong here. But he didn't want to discourage Ellie's obvious satisfaction at her idea, so he didn't say anything.

"This way," murmured Ellie, tugging the sleeve of Endymion's tunic. She led him through the kitchen and out the back door into the chilly night. An almost-full moon hung low over the rooftops, bathing Woolfold in pale light.

Leland was waiting. His light brown hair caught the moonlight. Ellie stiffened slightly beside Endymion.

"Well done, Ellie," said Leland. Endymion felt her reaction rather than saw it—tense, silent, expectant.

"Endymion," said Leland, "let's get you away from the house." He took Endymion's arm lightly.

Ellie seemed to feel herself dismissed. She faded back through the doorway as if she were fleeing the moonlight.

"Is this a good idea?" Endymion whispered.

Leland didn't respond to the question directly. He led Endymion to a spot where the moonlight pooled around a small pile of gear.

"A bedroll," he said, handing it to Endymion. "A backpack." He lifted that as well. "Ellie made you a good supply of food. Stuff that should last."

"Maybe I should have just stayed in the root cellar," said Endymion.

Leland met Endymion's gaze. "I never knew Oswin," he said. "He was only my half-brother, and he died before I was born." His head lowered, like the weight of being his father's least-favored son was pressing it down, "But my father's obsessed with him." His brow furrowed, "It's like he thinks punishing you will redeem him for Oswin's death."

Endymion didn't respond. He just met Leland's gaze.

Leland turned back to the pile of gear. "And," he said, "the crowning touch." He handed Endymion his pocket.

Endymion grabbed the familiar sheepskin pouch and clutched it to his chest like a scrap of home. "How'd you get it?" he asked. "Did my mother give it to you?"

Leland shook his head. "I'm afraid not," he said, a little sheepishly. "I snuck in when she wasn't at home." He put his hand on Endymion's shoulder. "I'm sorry to do this to you," he said, "but I really don't trust my father not to do something crazy." He gave Endymion a gentle shove. "Now go."

He turned and started back toward the house.

"Wait, Leland," Endymion called softly. "About Ellie's trick with the lock—It'll make them think that the fae…"

But Leland was already gone.

Endymion strapped the bedroll to the backpack, shouldered the pack, and tied his pocket around his waist. The gleaming light of the gibbous moon was bright enough that he didn't bother checking the pack for a lamp or tinderbox.

As he walked down the packed dirt road toward the trails that led up into the mountains, Endymion tried to make sense of what was happening. For a moment, he felt pressure at the corners of his eyes, like an untended dam about to break. But he shook his head and pulled himself together. His mother's wise—and sometimes too frequently stated—words came back to him: "If you don't card the wool, it's rough and tangled. But card it, spin it true, and you'll have cloth strong enough to weather whatever the world may bring."

The cool night air dried the moisture in his eyes, and his mind cleared a little, like mist lifting from a hillside. Endymion looked around at the cottages and sheepfolds of his little town as he walked toward the mountains—and whatever fate awaited him. His and Leland's houses were already behind him, but Lena's home and the simple cottage where Ellie's parents lived were closer. He couldn't shake a sense of dread—the feeling that he was looking at these humble cottages for the last time.

The trail leading up into the mountains was a little darker than the wider road between the houses in Woolfold. Still, the moonlight was on Endymion's side, and the trail was familiar. He took the same path that Calliope, Urania, and the other members of the flock had trodden so often. It almost felt like the path itself was one of the flock.

Somewhere between Leland's house and the base of the trail, he had come up with a purpose, a destination, and a plan.

The purpose wasn't surprising. It'd been the same since he and Lily were separated. He had to find her.

The destination—just as obvious—came from the purpose. Lily was in Greymoss Rest. He had to get there.

The plan—even Endymion could see—was full of holes. He didn't know where Greymoss Rest was, except in some general sense. He didn't know how long it might take him to find it. And he didn't even know where—or if—he'd lay his bedroll tonight.

T he moon was still spreading its light across the slopes when Endymion reached the meadow where he and Lily had met—what seemed like an eternity ago—and shared the happiest few weeks of his life, breaking bread beneath the open sky.

Endymion was no stranger to the night. In a simple village in the mountains, you had to be comfortable finding your way by moonlight or candlelight. But living near the hills and valleys around Woolfold also meant knowing the dangers the dark could hold. If he ran into a family of wolves—or worse, a bear—in the moonlight, he had no real defense. His sling was useless if the animal was too close or if he couldn't see it. His whittling knife might serve in an emergency, but it was no match for a wolf's teeth—or a bear's claws. And as his recent encounter with Thudwhack had shown, there could be worse things in the dark than animals.

Several times during the long, cold hike up the trail, Endymion heard noises in the undergrowth. The darkness made every sound sharper, and every unseen creature seem larger than life.

It was a relief to reach the comforting familiarity of the meadow. Though the moon was still casting its cool, welcome glow, it was sinking dangerously close to the horizon.

Endymion found a spot behind a bush at the base of the stone escarpment at the top of the dell, and spread his bedroll between the rock and the underbrush. It was the same spot where he'd once hidden to spy on the Wee Folk girl—who had, in fact, been spying on him.

The place, his meadow—where he had met Lily—felt like it had been waiting for him. As he got into his bedroll, he felt welcomed and safe. He pulled the amber amulet from his tunic. In the last glimmer of moonlight, it looked golden. He rubbed the smooth surface. A warmth that felt like Lily's breath, but was probably just his own body heat, flowed from the medallion into his fingers.

"Lily," he said quietly, speaking to the shining amulet, "I'd gladly sleep a hundred years, if I could waken to see you."

Endymion woke before the sun—or at least before it burned through the gray mist cloaking the meadow. The sun was there, somewhere. The mist glowed softly, making the morning look like a sheet with a candle flickering somewhere behind it.

He opened his backpack for the first time to see what Leland and Ellie had packed for him. Curious, he rummaged through the contents and nodded appreciatively. The pack seemed to hold what he might need. The tinderbox and small lamp he had nearly reached for the night before were there, along with as much food as the pack could carry. There was dried fruit and salted meat. He was glad to see a tightly wrapped packet of traveling bread. It was dense and kept well, but it looked like Ellie had spread mulberry preserve across the upper crust. Endymion's mouth watered at the thought. Tucked between the bread and salted meat was a lump of hard cheese wrapped in waxed cloth.

At the bottom of the pack lay a spool of thin rope and a cloth square that could serve many purposes. One of them, he thought with a flicker of unease, was to bind a wound. He hoped *that* use of the cloth wouldn't be needed.

There was a pair of wool socks as well—hand-knit, by the look of them. It occurred to Endymion that he couldn't imagine a kinder jailer than Ellie. Not many jailers knit socks.

Endymion sighed, rolled up his bedroll, and shouldered the pack. He looked around the mist-shrouded clearing. It felt like he was still nestled in a woolen blanket. The fog felt warm now, though he imagined it would start to feel cold and clammy as he hiked—if the sun didn't burn it off. Those wool socks Ellie had provided might well come in handy.

It felt like the clearing was holding its breath, waiting for something. Not just something—someone. The place was waiting for Lily to arrive and brighten the morning with her fiery presence. This place, and Lily's presence in it, had reshaped his heart. It held a hole that could only be filled by finding her.

"All right," said Endymion to himself. "If I'm going to go off and get lost in the trees and rocks of the mountains, I might as well get to it." He started walking toward the place where the Wee Folk trail had been—before they erased it. "There's no sense in woolgathering."

The Woolfold in the Dell Moot met in the church nave. Some among them—mostly followers of the old ways who still believed Pan walked with them in the high hills —thought it unseemly to mix the Moot and the church, but it was the only building with enough room.

Villagers were welcome to attend, though not to speak —at least not until the Calling of the Green Commons, that brief moment when audience participation, though limited, was allowed.

Helen sat in the front row, eyeing her fellow villagers in their traditional Moot wear. In addition to the crimson robes— most of which Helen had woven herself—they wore a series of high hats, each more ridiculous than the last, at least in Helen's opinion. This culminated in the unbalanced high Mootcap worn by Mr. Branhelm—the Voice himself—its absurd height nearly brushing the rafters above the nave. Helen was astonished that he could balance it.

He was speaking—or pontificating, perhaps. "Now you all know me," he was saying. "A modest, humble man." Helen nearly snorted but managed to restrain herself. "I wouldn't presume to tell this esteemed, noble assembly what to think."

Helen glanced at the members of the Moot. Noble and esteemed felt a bit off the mark. Mr. Colwyk—Godric's pet smith —was staring at him like he was looking at the face of God. The other members of the assembly didn't seem too different. Helen searched the faces for a trace of critical thought—and found it hard to come by.

"But," continued Mr. Branhelm, "we have hard, incontrovertible evidence that the Fae have come to our village, even into our midst, and used their vile, ungodly magic to rescue one who, we must assume, is now one of their own."

A murmur rose from the crowd—not just the members of the assembly but the villagers in the pews as well.

Helen looked around at her fellow villagers—not just the ones in the red robes, but those sitting beside her in the pews. She despaired. The Calling of the Green Commons was coming. She would speak—she had to—but would it do any good? These people were superstitious, uneducated, and already buyers of what Godric was selling. She would plead for her son's life, soul, and future—but she could already see it would fall on deaf ears.

ndymion was already lost. When he tried to recall anything from his frantic run along the Wee Folk trail—from Thudwhack's cave to Greymoss Rest—all he could picture was a blur, the details smeared away. The path, the landmarks—everything that might have helped him find his way—was gone from his memory.

Even the mountains ahead—the same peaks that he'd seen rising above his village his whole life—felt unfamiliar, giving him a vague sense of disorientation and a low ache behind the eyes. One moment, he felt sure that he was heading toward Sheep's End, one of the higher peaks in the range directly to the east of Woolfold in the Dell, but when he looked down to check his footing, and looked up again, the peak directly in front of him looked more like Gray Mither—much farther to the north than the wrong end of the sheep.

Strangely enough—and Endymion had already tested it —when he turned around and tried to retrace his steps back toward Woolfold in the Dell, it felt easy. He could easily spot Puddingtop, the low mountain just to the southwest of Woolfold, and he knew exactly how to get back to the familiar trails.

It was a mystery. For a moment, he wondered if Fae magic was clouding his thoughts—twisting his sense of direction. But he shoved the thought aside. Lily would never let that happen. She was real. She was true. And she would want him to find her.

He'd come to believe the Wee Folk weren't so different from his own people—just smaller, quieter, a little stranger in their ways. Lily most of all. She was warm and solid in his arms, curious and clever, and when he kissed her—

Endymion shook his head and started walking again. He

had formed a tactic—though he wasn't sure it was working: veering a little right and left until he was heading in the direction that felt the most confusing, that made him feel the most lost. It was unpleasant, and each step made his head ache a little more, but he had no better idea, and Lily was waiting.

Helen looked at Marj beseechingly. "He's my son, Marj," she pleaded. "I don't know where he is." There was a whisper of wetness clinging to her eyelashes. "I don't know if he's alive, I don't know if he's with the Wee Folk." Her jaw clenched. "Ram's Teeth! I'm not even sure I know exactly who he is anymore." She blinked hard, and met Marj's eyes. "He got that amulet from somewhere, and he didn't tell me about it. What else didn't he tell me?"

Marj shook her head slowly, as if shaking off any doubts about who Endymion was. "Endymion's a good boy," she put her hand gently over Helen's. "You needn't have any fears on that account." Her tone sharpened. "I won't say the same for our Godric. I told him that those 'Fae' traces weren't real, certainly weren't magical, but would he listen?" She paused, then continued. "Why would you consult with an expert if you don't bother to listen to what she says?"

"Did he get the amulet from the Fae?" said Helen, her voice unsteady. "Did he eat of the Fairy fruit? When he was asking me about it, was it because he'd already been sampling it? Have the fairies seduced my son away from me?"

"My understanding," said Marj calmly, "is that the Wee Folk are just people—who really aren't that different from us. They have a different culture, probably originally came from some different place, but, though small, they are just another group of human beings." She looked up and met Helen's eyes. "I have this on the best authority. It's cunning folk knowledge—passed from mentor to student.

"The Wee Folk have magic, it's true," Marj continued. She held out her hand palm upward, and her brows knitted a little in concentration. "But so do we." She grunted, and a little flicker of fire—no bigger than a firefly—appeared above her palm, glowed a moment, then vanished with an acrid smell and a small, sharp hiss of smoke. A sudden chill crept through the room.

"But the Fae?" asked Helen.

"The Fae are just superstition," said Marj with a shake of her head. "The people we call the Wee Folk have different traditions, different magic, and a different culture, but they don't come from some magical realm. They're people, not unlike us, and anything else is misguided hogwash. And the sooner folk stop believing it, the better."

Endymion was exhausted. It was his second day of struggling against his own sense of direction. The day before, he'd followed his tactic—letting confusion guide him, hoping what felt most like the wrong direction was the right one. When it got dark he'd barely managed to unroll his bedroll and eat a little food from his pack before passing out beneath a scraggly pine tree.

In the morning, he'd eaten another of Ellie's traveling breads. As he licked the mulberry preserve off his lip, he realized how tired he'd been the night before. The bread was delicious, and made him appreciate Ellie's gentle custody anew. The night before, he'd wolfed it down without tasting it.

By noon, the constant back and forth and fighting through the underbrush had left him sweaty and cold at the same time, his head feeling like it could split open. He stopped at a point where he could sit on some rocks and look out over the foothills toward Woolfold in the Dell. Looking back home, the ache in his head lessened, if only a little.

Endymion considered despairing, as if it were a choice he could take or leave. He had no idea if he was going in the right direction. He had no idea how long it would take him to get to Greymoss Rest even if he was walking true. He had a pretty good idea how welcome he would be once he got there, if he made it. The answer, of course, was: not at all.

Endymion considered despairing, but then he rejected the thought. Lily was waiting for him. It didn't matter how unwelcoming Sorrel and Blossom had been the last time, Lily was there—so Greymoss Rest was where he had to go.

After a brief rest and a refreshing drink from a cool mountain stream, Endymion resumed his journey. As the afternoon wore on, a flicker of hope returned. Even though his exhaustion didn't ease, he felt—somehow—that he was making some progress.

Each time he tried to determine which way to go, using his lack of guidance as a guide, he felt like there was some barrier obscuring the proper choice. It felt as if, with his persistence, he was wearing that barrier thin. As if each turn was scraping away at the skin of a great bubble of misdirection that surrounded Greymoss Rest, and it was about to pop. It was like something inside himself was pulling him forward, pulling him toward wherever Lily was.

Endymion stepped into a glade. The sun was starting to approach the horizon. He paused, wondering whether this would be a good place to make camp. Then he heard the sound of something coming through the trees on the other side of the clearing.

A large, lumbering manlike figure broke through the trees and pushed its way into view. A brutish face turned toward Endymion.

He knew that face.

Thudwhack.

T hudwhack spotted him. Endymion froze. The ogre almost comically scratched his head. He muttered to himself—at least he might have thought of it as muttering, but the sound boomed clearly across the green field between them. It seemed the ogre didn't have an inside voice.

"Thudwhack told not eat little ones," he thunder-muttered.

Endymion hesitated. His choices were to bolt or stay frozen. So far staying frozen had kept Thudwhack from moving toward him—and he liked that dynamic. He kept still.

Thudwhack peered at Endymion. Again, it was almost painfully easy to read the thoughts moving across his face, but as if to make it even clearer, he kept talking. "This not little one," the ogre said decisively. "This middle one." He took his first lumbering step into the clearing.

That was enough for Endymion. He turned and bolted into the underbrush back the way he'd come.

He was short of breath almost immediately. He'd already been exhausted from his daily battles with his own disorientation. On the plus side, he was running away from Greymoss Rest, so his headache got better, and he knew which way home was.

There was the thundering sound of massive footsteps not far behind him. Thudwhack was close on his tail. The ogre wasn't fast—either mentally or physically—but each of his strides was worth at least two of Endymion's. Trying to outrun him in a straight line was a lost cause even before it began.

Endymion ducked and weaved, cutting through the underbrush as fast as his laboring lungs allowed. For a time the crashing sounds behind him were near, then they gradually got further away, as he found narrow places—gaps between rocks and tangles of knotted trees—that were harder for the ogre to navigate.

The sun had already been setting when Endymion had set foot into the clearing. It was getting dark enough that he could barely see where to plant his feet.

Endymion took a wrong step—there was a crunch as his ankle twisted in a direction it wasn't meant to go. He plummeted to the ground, hit his head, and watched as the last faint glimmers of the setting sun faded into an unyielding, unconscious darkness.

M r. Colwyk was standing at his anvil, wearing his smith's apron. He pounded his hammer down on a piece of glowing iron. The small fragment of metal was gradually taking the shape of a horseshoe under the unerring rhythmic blows.

The sound of the hammer strikes was quite irritating to Tilda Pratt, who was leaning awkwardly—one might almost say perching—on the open half-door to the smithy. She was trying to speak to Mr. Colwyk, but was finding competing with the hammer's pounding to be quite challenging.

"Godric," she said. The hammer went **Clang**.

"Won't—" **Clank**.

"Tell—" she squawked. The hammer slammed into the metal again. **Bang**.

"Me—" **KLANG!**

"What—he's—*planning*!" she blurted out. Even though that last word had burst out louder than she intended, she preened, pleased with herself for having scrabbled the sentence past the din.

Mr. Colwyk reluctantly lowered his hammer. He glared accusingly at the incomplete horseshoe, and then at Mrs. Pratt.

"Well," he said, "Should he?" He looked askance at the awkward woman in black perched on his half-open half-door. "You're not a Mootsman. You weren't part of the Moot's private discussion." He shook his head. "Anyway. Even I don't know exactly what he's up to. He asked the Moot's permission to deal with the problem as he saw fit." He gave his cooling horseshoe a rueful glance. "Some of the Mootsmen were reluctant, but I'm sure Godric will do the right thing."

"But," said Tilda, "I was there from the beginning! I'm the

one who told him in the first place!" Her voice was rising as she spoke, until it neared a screech. "If it weren't for me, no one would have even known that Endymion was eating the fairy fruit!"

Tilda paused, as if realizing how loud that last sentence had been. She glanced up and down the street to see if anyone other than Mr. Colwyk was listening.

"Well, good for you," said the smith tiredly. He grabbed his tongs, picked up the twisted little piece of metal, and looked at it skeptically.

Endymion woke—face pressed to the ground—to the song of a skylark, bright and bubbling as it sailed overhead. The joyful sound washed over him like a wave. Then his lips parted slightly, and he tasted the moss and dirt where he lay. He tried to sit up—and a jolting pain in his ankle reminded him not only that he was alive but also that he would die someday. And just now, that day didn't seem so far off.

For a moment, the despair he'd been wrestling with only yesterday came back. Then he thanked his lucky stars. Yes, he was alone in the mountains. Yes, he probably wasn't going to be able to walk, at least today. Yes, he was also eating dirt. But—on the positive side—and Endymion considered this a *very* positive side—he hadn't ended up as an ogre's dinner. All the running he'd done the previous evening before he'd ended up here must have shaken the ogre off his trail.

Endymion pushed himself up to a sitting position—pain flaring in his ankle—and looked around to plan his morning. First things first, he pulled off his shoe and sock and rolled his leggings up to examine the injury. His ankle was swollen and discolored. Where his foot had twisted between a tree root and the ground, the skin had split, and it was covered with grit and dirt.

Endymion had reason to consider himself blessed again. He needed to clean the wound, and he needed water to drink. And, just below the morning birdsong that still trilled in the treetops, he could hear the trickle of a mountain stream.

There were lots of little streams running down the slopes of the mountains. They all made their way, eventually, to the Dragon River, which flowed down the west side of Liamec from the Serpent's Gorge in the south through the Western Reaches all the way to the fabled ocean in the north. From Helen's stories, he'd gotten the impression that she had seen that mighty body of water. He certainly never had.

Endymion made his way, painfully, slowly, to find the stream. In another stroke of good fortune, it wasn't far, though he was panting and sweating from the pain by the time he got there.

First, he drank greedily, then he cleaned his ankle as best he could, grimacing with the pain each time he touched it. When he pulled the piece of cloth from the bottom of the backpack and used it to bind up the wound—trying to make the binding tight enough to support the ankle—he couldn't help but remember hoping that the multi-purpose cloth wouldn't end up used for this purpose.

GREYMOSS REST

Marj picked up her cup of chamomile tea and took a sip. The straw-colored liquid darkened the rim of the wooden cup as a faint slurping sound broke the stillness in the air. "I used to go there, you know," she said quietly.

"There?" asked Helen.

"Greymoss Rest," said Marj, "the healing woman there..." she paused. "You'd likely call her an herbalist. They called her their Herbmother." She touched the bridge of her nose, a gesture that made her look deep in thought. "Her name was Sorrel. She and I used to be friends."

They were sitting at the table in Helen's house. Marj had come to see how she was faring—there had been no word from Endymion in several days.

"Was there much contact between the two villages?" asked Helen.

Marj shook her head. "Not that much. A little trade. As far as I know, I was the only one who went there for social reasons." She frowned, the corners of her mouth trying to negotiate the border between anger and sadness. "Well—except for Oswin and Tomlin.

"That was before the trail disappeared." Her expression darkened. "Before the Red Spring... I've tried to go back a few times." The head shake this time was as much frustration as it was denial. "It wasn't possible. It's too bad. I liked Sorrel. I was learning a lot from her—about herbs, about the Wee Folk."

"So they're not bad people?" asked Helen, her voice catching a little. "They won't be cruel to my Endymion?"

Marj gave a small shrug. "No," she said. "They're not bad people." She crossed her arms. "Truth be told, after the Red Spring, we're the ones folks should be wary of—not them."

E ndymion spent the morning testing whether he could get some use out of his injured ankle. He loosened the binding, then strapped a tree branch to it, but even a little weight made his whole leg throb, sharp and insistent—more than he could bear.

He tried crawling, hopping, and even walking with a stout stick as a crutch, but nothing helped him move more than a few feet away from his lifeline—the stream.

With travel out of the question—at least for now—Endymion removed the cloth from his ankle and rinsed it in the trickling water. As he bound up his injury again, the reddening around the edges of the wound worried him. He'd heard that strong spirits could keep a wound from rot, but he had nothing like that to pour on his ankle.

He ate sparingly from the provisions Leland and Ellie had left him, mindful they might have to last. He blessed again the fortune that had made Ellie his jailer. Her traveling bread was the best he'd ever had—except for the magical memories of the lunches he'd shared with Lily. He was careful not to miss a crumb or a drop of the mulberry preserve.

With the realization that he wasn't going far—or even anywhere—today, Endymion set about making his spot by the stream as livable as the small glade allowed. He was able to hobble about the little clearing as long as he avoided putting any weight on his ankle.

The site, at least, had its advantages. The running stream provided clear, cool water; he found a spot between two boulders where he could lie, somewhat sheltered from the rain if the weather were to shift in that direction, and he was even able to clear a workable firepit among the stones nearby.

Endymion debated lighting a fire. It might keep him warm—maybe even alive—but it could also give away his hiding place. And if someone came?

It might be help. It might be Thudwhack.

In the end, Endymion chose to gather wood for a fire. Fortunately, there were wind-weathered mountain trees all around the clearing that had become his home. Unfortunately, limping around to collect the fallen branches and tree limbs was both painful and exhausting.

When Endymion finally sank into his rocky alcove, the fire had become an afterthought. He slept the deep, dreamless rest of one under the watchful eye of Hypnos, the god of sleep— and perhaps Hades, the god of death, as well.

Ewan sat on his usual stool at the alehouse. He hadn't been back since Endymion went missing. He wasn't a regular—not really—but now and then, at the end of his day, he'd stop in for an ale before heading home to Helen and Endymion.

The alehouse common room was dark, with rough wooden beams running across the ceiling. Ewan usually sat at one end of the counter and quietly drank his ale. Today, he was drawing more attention than usual.

John, the miller, sidled over from the other end of the counter, shifting awkwardly from one three-legged stool to the next until he reached Ewan's. Ewan had watched this performance out of the corner of his eye, hoping against all odds to be left alone with his ale.

John looked at Ewan and said, "Your Endymion's done gone and put his foot in it, hasn't he?" He followed this with the gesture every sheep farmer knew—pantomiming flicking a dag, a dried bit of sheep dung, off his hand.

Ewan grunted. The grunt could have been interpreted as noncommittal, and indeed, John seemed to take it that way.

Behind the counter, the aleman Martin heard the grunt differently. In that sound, he heard a rising tide of anger—quiet, unrelenting. Martin shook his head sharply, trying to catch John's eye. But John—characteristically—was oblivious.

"Our Godric's got it," said John, with a smile that carried a hint of a sneer. "He'll get it sorted." He looked knowingly at Ewan. "He'll have a plan. It'll be just like the Red Spring."

Martin leaned across the counter and set a hand on John's shoulder. "Well, that's enough for you, mate," he said. "I'm cutting you off." He squinted at John. "You're what—twenty-five?" He gave a faint shake of his head. "Just a kid watching the soldiers that spring, weren't you?"

Ewan got up from his stool and took one more swig from his ale cup. He grunted an acknowledgment to Martin, nodded, and without a glance at John, walked out.

When Endymion woke, he thought the sun was beating down on his brow. When he reached a finger to his forehead, it came away wet with clammy sweat. But his spot between the two rocks was shaded, and the morning air felt cool.

He struggled to his feet—or as near as he could manage. His ankle was worse. It had stiffened up overnight—he couldn't flex it at all.

After battling his way to the stream, he drank deeply from the chill water. It tasted like the icy peaks of the mountains. Then, he set about the unpleasant task of removing the bandage on his ankle and doing what little he could to tend it.

Endymion gritted his teeth and got to it. It wasn't made any easier by the fact that each touch to the ankle or tender skin around the cut would send sharp pains shooting through his leg.

His ankle, foot, and lower leg were swollen and bruised —purple, blue, and yellow radiating out from the wound. The break in the skin was red and inflamed. It wasn't bleeding anymore, but Endymion had seen wounds fester on the sheep, and he knew the signs. He didn't have the faintest idea what to do. Back home, there'd have been no question: He'd have gone to Marj, who almost certainly would've had a potion or some kind of ointment to help.

He cleaned the wound as best he could with cold stream water.

With his injury tended, Endymion thought about his options. He wasn't going anywhere, that was for sure. Not today, and not tomorrow, either. He could eat. He could try to improve his little shelter. But there wasn't much else to do. Tonight, he would light his little fire and make it burn as brightly as possible.

Maybe someone was looking for him and would see the light. It felt like his only hope.

The thought came again—what if Thudwhack saw the fire? But at this point, Endymion almost didn't care. Even Thudwhack was better than being forgotten.

Endymion reached under his tunic and wrapped his fingers around the amber amulet with Lily's hair inside. The touch steadied him—like grasping Lily's hand.

T he wind rattled the shutters, each gust echoing through the empty loft. Helen reached to secure the wooden crossbar, hoping it would quiet the noise. The storm was coming in from the west, but today the winds reached greedy fingers around to the other sides of the cottage.

She'd been adjusting the windows to keep out as much weather as she could. Like most houses in the village, hers had no west-facing windows. It was something of a rule, unwritten but deeply understood. If you wanted your home to be livable, you closed the west side to the wind.

The loft was a tight space. As Helen stretched to grasp the crossbar, Endymion's cot shifted just enough to uncover a glimpse of something pale beneath it—white and yellow, like captured sunlight.

She reached under the bed and drew out a dried garland made of daisies. It had been under there for days—perhaps weeks. Some of the petals had begun to fall, but the weave of the stems still held as she lifted it.

Helen's breath caught. She stared at the garland, searching for a clue to Endymion's whereabouts among the fading daisy petals.

She turned it in her hands, gauging its size. Too small for Endymion. She carefully tried it on herself—too small for her, too. She wondered who it might have been meant for—whose head was small enough for it to fit?

She sat very still, the garland resting like a bird in her lap, as the wind sang through the shutters. The storm outside raged on, but it was the silence inside that undid her.

Helen began to cry. The little garland—so small, so lovingly crafted—made it suddenly, sharply real. Her boy was gone. Not just out of reach but lost to the wilds, to silence, to fear. And she didn't know when—or if—she'd see him again.

Endymion woke in a shallow pool of rainwater. The storm had crashed and thundered above his sheltering rocks all night, leaving his hollow filled with clammy water. Perhaps *woke* wasn't quite the right word—he drifted into awareness in a feverish haze rather than true waking.

He pulled himself out from under the rocks, shivering and sweating in turns. Thirst wasn't his first need—he had to warm his chilled body, or he feared he might not wake again.

The storm had broken with the dawn, and warm sunlight was beginning to reach the clearing. Endymion dragged his aching, sluggish body onto a higher patch of ground where the sun had warmed the earth. With a final shudder, he collapsed —and sleep claimed him again, easing his pain with the quiet fading of thought.

* * *

When Endymion next surfaced, fever still clouding his thoughts, he wasn't sure if it was later that same day—or the next.

He crawled to the stream and took a few sips of cool mountain water. Glancing at the stained cloth wrapped around his ankle, he forced down a few bites of the travel bread. His appetite had vanished, and rationing no longer seemed to matter.

Endymion looked at his firepit. The effort of trying to light a fire didn't just seem like too much, it seemed like an impossibility.

He slipped back into his nest under the overhanging rocks, and stumbled into unconsciousness as if tripping over the edge of waking—and falling in.

T he soldiers marched into town—two rows of armed men, ten in a row. It wasn't many men—not really—but oh, how their shiny weapons glinted in the early sun—and how neatly and cleanly they marched, in perfect step.

They must have set up camp the evening before, just outside of town—to be here as dawn was breaking through the clouds. It was clear the captain wanted to make an impression on the locals. He rode a magnificent horse at the head of the column. Young, proud, and alert. There was no way he was old enough to know anything about the Red Spring—let alone care.

Each man wore his polished chain mail, and held a gleaming spear. The weapons and armor caught the sunlight. Over their chain mail, they wore brown tabards with a black silhouette of a stag—the mark of the baron of the western marches, the man who ruled the lands on the western side of the kingdom of Liamec, subject only to the king in Capitol.

One of the two men marching in the first row—just behind the captain on his horse—carried a tall banner of brown fabric, emblazoned with that same silhouette, the image of the noble stag rising over the troop, leading them forward.

The baron was known for the discipline and order of his troops. If this young captain's supervisors were here, they would be unable to fault him. The uniforms and armor were clean and well-maintained. The men marched like cogs in a well-oiled machine. It looked like a military parade.

And to the children of Woolfold in the Dell, it might as well have been one. From across the village they gathered, and lined the streets. In silence, mostly, though occasionally one would break ranks and gasp, cheer, or inappropriately titter, they watched the lines of brown-clad men march into the village. This was a spectacle unlike anything they had seen before.

Their elders stayed inside. A shutter lifted here, a rough wool curtain moved aside slightly there, but no one came out into the morning sun to confront, question, or even greet this invasion.

The captain rode up to one of the older children, reined in his splendid horse, and called out to the boy on the ground beneath him, "Show me the way to your village leader."

The boy froze under the unexpected attention, and stuttered a bit as he tried to answer. "You mean Mr. Branhelm, Your Worship?"

The captain frowned. "I don't know. Don't care. I need someone to talk to—someone who can tell me why we're here."

Endymion was in heaven. He was relieved to finally be here. The journey had been both difficult and painful. His brow was cool, the pain in his ankle was distant—less sharp—and best of all, Lily was here. He heard her humming the melody of one of the songs she had sung to him back in their meadow.

Something worried him, though. Why was Lily here? If she was in heaven with him, that meant she was dead too—and he didn't want Lily to be dead. He forced his eyes open.

She was there, leaning over him, mopping his brow with a damp cloth.

"There you are," she said quietly, a little catch in her voice. "I thought I might have lost you."

Endymion stared at her, taking in the vision. She looked as beautiful as ever, though her hair was tangled, and her brow was beaded with sweat as well. He parted his lips to speak—nothing but a croak emerged.

Lily took advantage of his open mouth to ease the neck of a waterskin between his teeth. She squeezed the skin, and a trickle of cool water crossed his tongue. He coughed and spluttered, but the water soothed his throat and calmed his thirst.

"You've made a right good mess of things, haven't you?" said Lily, half-scolding. Tears welled in her eyes.

"Lily?" he rasped.

"Aye," she said. "It's me." She shook her head. "Though I don't know why I bothered. You're obviously more trouble than you're worth." A teardrop made its way to the corner of her eye, and trickled down her flushed cheek. If Endymion had been strong enough, he would have reached up and brushed it away with his finger.

He became aware of where he was: lying in the sun on the high place just outside his little rock shelter. Something was underneath him—an improvised stretcher. His bedroll cloth had been stretched between two thick branches from nearby trees. It was bound together with string or twine that looked like Wee Folk fabric. The stretcher was big enough to carry him, though clearly meant to be dragged—by someone far smaller.

"Lily," he said, "you can't."

"It's not a matter of whether I can or can't," replied the Wee Folk woman, "I have to."

When Endymion next awoke, it was to the scrape and rumble of the stretcher over rough ground. He was lying on his back, facing away from Lily. He couldn't see her, but he could hear her. Each lurching inch drew a ladylike groan from the Wee Folk woman. Each jolt also caused a pain in his leg that burned like fire, but Endymion was damned if he was going to add that to Lily's list of worries.

The pain was making him nauseated, though he knew his stomach was empty. Endymion shook his head to clear the fog clouding his thoughts. The fresh air outside his rock shelter, and perhaps the pain shooting up his spine, helped a bit, cutting through the haze.

He turned his head as far as he could, trying to catch a glimpse of Lily. All he could make out was the straps looped from her shoulders to the stretcher. It looked like she'd ingeniously used his backpack to fashion a makeshift harness.

"Lily," he croaked.

Endymion felt a shaking as Lily freed herself from the straps and lowered the end of the stretcher to the ground. Her face appeared between him and the sky. It was flushed red, dripping sweat, and smeared with grime. He'd never seen anything more beautiful.

"Thank you, Endymion," said Lily, breathlessly, "I was ready for a break. Very thoughtful of you to notice."

"Lily," said Endymion. "How did you find me?"

"Something to drink first," said Lily. She unfastened a water flask from the stretcher's side, held it to Endymion's cracked lips, and dribbled a splash of water into his mouth. Then, she took a healthy swig herself.

She shook her head, her dusty copper braids bouncing

across her face. "'No one knows the paths of the soul-threaded, only that they always lead to one another.'" She poured a little water on the hem of her tunic and wiped the sweat from Endymion's brow. "My father used to say that. I never quite knew what it meant." She frowned. "I still don't understand it—but now I believe it."

Lily blinked, and looked directly into Endymion's eyes. "A few days ago, I knew you needed me. At first, I didn't know where to look. Out here, I found that walking in certain directions felt right."

Endymion smiled faintly. "I'm glad."

"Me too," Lily whispered.

With a quiet, graceful grunt, which Endymion thought was among the sweetest sounds he'd ever heard—the stretcher lurched back into motion. The movement sent another surge of pain running up his body from his leg. He bit back a cry, forcing himself to silence. He didn't want to worry Lily, and if she heard him, she would almost certainly stop again.

He couldn't see her, but he thought a little casual conversation might ease the situation.

"Lily?" he said.

"Still here," she replied, panting. Her voice sounded right beside him, though hearing the lilting sound made him regret not seeing her face.

"How are you doing this?" he asked. "I must weigh twice what you do."

"Well," Lily began. Her tone reminded him of Helen patiently explaining—again—that Euripides and Eupolis were two entirely different people, despite the similarity of the names. "It would be a bit easier if I didn't have to waste my breath on explaining things." She let out another grunt as the stretcher's tail end bumped over a root or a rock.

"Sorry," Endymion murmured—and in that moment, he truly was. Sorry that he was being such a burden, sorry that his actions had caused such a ruckus back in Woolfold. Sorry that he was driving a wedge between Sorrel and Lily. But never sorry that he'd met Lily. Being sorry for that would be like being sorry for having been born.

"Oh," said Lily brightly. "It's not a problem." She muttered a curse word under her breath as she stumbled slightly. The word was one Endymion didn't know, though it sounded impressively rude. "I've been feeling like I needed a little exercise."

Endymion was silent. He didn't know if his attempt at conversation was helping, or hurting.

"We're almost to one of our trails," said Lily encouragingly. "That'll make the pulling a bit easier." She paused for a moment, breathing heavily. "And I took a couple of my mother's cordials from her stillroom—where she concocts her potions. One was the healing balm I've been spreading on your wound. The other was a strength elixir. Only little sips. I promise."

G odric Branhelm was thoroughly put out. The captain of the troop sent in response to his request for help was being uncooperative. For one, he had insisted Godric accompany them to Greymoss Rest; for another, he refused to say what he intended to do once they arrived.

Godric had reluctantly laced up his long-unused work boots and was now trudging through the hills—caught between a horse's backside and a column of soldiers. It was far beneath his usual habits—he was used to paying others for this kind of exertion.

The captain had asked Godric to find him the most qualified guide to lead them to the Wee Folk Village. He'd suggested Ned—the tanner's boy. He was known for exploring the mountain trails around Woolfold, and ran errands for all the folk in town. Godric had thought about making a joke about using Tilda Pratt to lead them, but the captain's sense of humor —if it existed—seemed even more deeply buried than Godric's own.

Ned strode alongside the captain's horse, his chest puffed with importance. He pointed eagerly at peaks and trails, rattling off names like a squire trying to impress his knight. The captain didn't respond—didn't even nod—but Ned didn't seem to notice. There was something about boys and soldiers: a natural pull, even when the admiration wasn't returned.

The soldiers marching in ranks behind Godric were disciplined and organized, the jangle and clatter of their gear nearly blending into a single sound with each step they took, even with twenty men in the line. Godric wondered if they were keeping such strict order because he and the boy were with them. He couldn't imagine that they could march for days that way.

He had worried that the rumored Wee Folk spell on the trail between Woolfold in the Dell and Greymoss Rest would make it hard—or even impossible—to find their way, but Ned and the captain seemed to be navigating the trails well. For a moment, Godric speculated that maybe the spell affected individuals, but not an entire troop of soldiers. He shook his head and pushed the thought aside. He didn't know anything about how Wee Folk magic worked—and had no intention of learning.

When Endymion next opened his eyes, he saw Sorrel leaning over him. He was so relieved—and happy—that he could have kissed her, but he settled for giving her the biggest smile he'd ever given anyone. His cheeks hurt.

Endymion didn't know it, but his smile had the unreserved joy of a six-month-old greeting someone they loved.

Sorrel was hard-pressed not to respond in kind. But she only frowned and said, "You're smiling like my wayward daughter didn't just drop two near-death patients on my doorstep."

"Two?" asked Endymion weakly, his relief turning instantly to panic. "Is Lily all right?"

Sorrel shook her head. "No daughter of mine would abuse a stamina cordial so recklessly." She pinched her lips together. "She's in the next bed," she said, gesturing behind her.

Endymion turned his head to look. Lily was lying there, her skin pale as a daisy petal. She had always been fair, her red hair making her complexion glow, but now her face looked shaped from moonlight. "Will she be all right?" he asked Sorrel, barely able to breathe.

Sorrel scowled. "With time. She misused the potion she took from my stillroom. You're never supposed to drink so much, and for so long. She burned through every shred of strength her body could spare. But, at this point she just needs rest. The same goes for you. I've applied the curatives you need to draw the fever-root from your wound, and splinted it, but you need time to heal as well."

Endymion glanced from Lily's cot to his, then back again. "I thought you were trying to keep us apart," he said.

For the first time, a hint of a smile touched Sorrel's face. "And you saw how well that worked out, didn't you?" she asked.

Endymion tried to reach out to Lily's cot, to touch her, but found his arm almost too weak to lift. Sorrel studied him for a moment, her face unreadable, then she reached out, caught his hand, and gently tucked his arm back under the blanket on his cot. "Sleep now," she said, placing her palm calmly on his forehead. Almost against his will, Endymion found his eyes closing, and felt Morpheus's veil of dream folding across his thoughts.

RED SPRING

T he sound of Lily's lilting language stirred Endymion from sleep. He sat up, more alert than he had felt in days. He hadn't been moved—he was still in the cot where he'd fallen asleep. Lily lay in the next one. The rhythmic rumble of her breath, soft and steady, brought him more comfort than he could have explained.

If she was sleeping, then what was he hearing? It sounded like Sorrel speaking softly in the next room. A deeper voice answered hers. They sounded tense—strained, maybe even angry.

Endymion listened for a moment. The voices were low, but sharp with feeling. He could hear them, but couldn't understand the words. Lily and Sorrel's tongue sounded musical and bright, yet completely alien. He did, however, make out the word Móra repeated several times. When the male voice said it, he spat it out like a curse.

Endymion looked around. The two cots were side by side in the middle of a large room. He guessed it was Sorrel's stillroom, her space for herb-work and healing. The walls were lined with shelves. Strings of herbs crisscrossed the low ceiling overhead. He realized that even if he could stand, he wouldn't be able to walk upright. The herbs dangled just within Sorrel's reach; he'd have to crouch—or even crawl—to move from one side of the room to another.

A well-used workbench at Sorrel's height, littered with vials, flasks, and various small tools, stood near the shelves. A metal cauldron sat against one wall. It reminded Endymion of Marj's alchemy workshop back in Woolfold.

The voices fell silent. Endymion heard a slamming door. Sorrel walked into the room.

"So, I see that at least one of my patients is awake," she said, her tone gentle. "Móra," she continued, with a nod to Endymion.

Remembering the contempt in the man's voice as he spat that word, Endymion met Sorrel's gaze as firmly as he could from where he lay.

"My name's Endymion," he said.

"Of course," said Sorrel. "You're right—and I'm sorry." She returned his gaze. "How are you feeling, Endymion?" she asked.

G odric watched as Ned, the tanner's boy, came bounding back down the slope. He called out to the captain. "I've found it," he said, gesturing frantically behind himself. "You can see it from the top of the ridge."

They had been wandering through the wood, their path growing less certain with each step. Godric had begun to wonder if the Wee Folk's rumored spell was having more effect than he'd thought.

The captain spurred his horse and rode ahead, the excited boy scrambling after him. The discipline of the men—so pronounced when they had left Woolfold—had eased a bit on the long march, especially as their confidence in Ned's sense of direction had wavered. Now, with their destination reportedly in sight, Godric saw straps being tightened, tunics being tucked in, and shields being unstrapped from backs.

The captain reached the ridgeline, the sun, just beginning to set, silhouetting horse and rider against the sky. He made a heroic figure. For a moment Godric could almost see why Ned looked up to him.

Godric crested the ridge himself, slightly winded, and saw what the captain and the tanner's boy were looking at.

A mountain dell was beneath them. Probably not more than half a mile away, the village, their destination, lay spread out below them like a map drawn by the duke's own cartographer.

It was darker in the depths of the dell than here atop the ridge, and it was a little hard to make out where streets began and ended. But the shapes of houses were visible. The streets, dark as they were, seemed to glimmer in the fading light. The village was encircled by a wooden wall. Godric noticed that the houses seemed oddly shaped, eerily so to him. *What didn't the Wee Folk, the Fae, do strangely—or wrongly?* A shudder rose up his spine.

"Well done, lad," said the captain to Ned. Ned straightened, shoulders squared like a knight standing before his king.

The captain turned to his men, also reaching the crest of the ridge. "All right, men," he said. "We'll set up camp here. No sense marching blindly in the dark. We'll approach the village in the morning."

Endymion sat up a little straighter on his cot. He met Sorrel's gaze. Lily's soothing breath rumbled quietly behind him. He wondered if it was as reassuring to Sorrel as it was to himself. "So, who was that, Sorrel?" he asked. "Who were you arguing with?"

"What?" replied the Wee Folk woman, unsure of herself for the first time since Endymion had known her.

"That man you were arguing with," continued Endymion. "I heard the word Móra. Whoever he was—he sounded angry."

Sorrel frowned. "Oran, the Taproot. He's at the heart of the circle this year." Endymion's confusion must have shown on his face, she softened her voice.

"We call our council the Rootcircle. A new center is appointed each year, called the Taproot. Oran guides us this year."

"So the village knows I'm here," said Endymion warily.

"They know," said Sorrel. "Lily was too weary to do more than collapse at the gate after dragging you here. They know, and they're not happy about it. But, for the moment, they can see that you both are in need of my care, and that overrides other concerns."

Endymion glanced over his shoulder. Lily hadn't stirred. A lock of hair had fallen across her cheek, and he fought the urge to brush it away.

"What are they planning to do with me?" he asked.

The sunlight coming in through the windows had turned ruddy, painting the shelves and the herbs tied above them in red shadow.

"They don't know," said Sorrel, her eyes searching his face. "I don't know," she continued. "What should we do with you, Endymion?" she asked. She rubbed the bridge of her nose and exhaled. She looked tired.

"Let me be with Lily," said Endymion, his voice steady.

"Let's talk about that tomorrow," said Sorrel, her expression softening. "It's late. You should get some sleep."

Morning sunlight glinted off the soldiers' polished spears as they marched into the clearing before the wooden gate. Wisps of early mist still clung to the trees, fading quickly in the rising sun. The forest seemed to be holding its breath; not a bird sang. The only sound was the shifting of armor and the scuff of the soldiers' boots on the grass.

The gate was closed. Flowering vines softened its appearance but did nothing to lessen the barrier it posed. There was no sign of any defenders.

Even the wind had gone quiet. The silence seemed to be deepening.

The captain turned to Godric. "You might have told me the village was fortified," he said, breaking the stillness.

Godric hesitated, eyes fixed on the wooden palisade. "It wasn't," he said quietly.

The captain studied the village gate. His eyes lingered on the vines and the carved wood. There was a faint smell of lavender in the air. "Even so," he murmured, "it doesn't look like a place bracing for war."

He nudged his horse a step forward. "Men," he called, "at the ready."

One of the younger soldiers adjusted his grip, his spearpoint wobbling slightly before he stilled it again. They all formed into a single long line, shields ready, spears at their sides. Godric swallowed. He'd never seen so many weapons in one place. The spears stood like leafless trees in winter—steady, waiting, unyielding.

The captain rode forward into the center of the clearing, midway between his line of armed men and the flower-adorned palisade. He scanned the treetops before turning his gaze back to the gate. His expression was unreadable. He touched the hilt of his sword but did not draw it.

"People of Graymoss," he called out. He glanced back at Godric. "Graymoss, right?" he asked in a quieter voice.

"Greymoss Rest," said Godric. His mouth was dry.

"People of Greymoss Rest," the captain resumed, his voice rising.

"*You are summoned to answer!*"

Endymion was in a happy place again. For a moment, he couldn't say what made him so sure it was a good place —then he realized that it was because Lily was there. Anyplace with Lily in it was paradise for him.

"Endymion," she said urgently, "you've got to wake up! The soldiers are here."

He opened his eyes—reluctantly—to find her hovering over him. She looked pale but alert. His heart surged with joy at the sight of her.

"Soldiers?" he asked groggily.

"From Woolfold in the Dell," said Lily.

Endymion sat up. "There aren't any soldiers in Woolfold in the Dell," he said.

Lily shook her head. "It doesn't matter where they're from," she said. "I think they're here because of us. We have to go out there and help!"

Endymion tried to rise—then ran into two problems. The herbs strung overhead were brushing the top of his head when he sat up, and there was a heavy and awkward splint on his leg.

He shifted his weight to see how his ankle held up and felt a low, dull ache, not the sharp, shooting pain he expected.

Lily helped him crawl from the bed to the door of the stillroom. The ache in his ankle was more manageable than he had feared. The next room's ceiling wasn't higher, but there weren't any lines of dried herbs cutting across it. Endymion was able to stand, though his head nearly touched the wood. The air was cooler here, and a shaft of early light stretched across the smooth-grained wooden floor.

Lily handed Endymion a pair of rough wooden crutches. He studied them for a moment before slipping them under his arms. The handholds, knobbed ends, and curved armrests looked grown rather than cut. They felt as though they had been made specifically for him. Standing, even with the crutches, he felt unsteady—but there wasn't time for that now.

"This way," said Lily, opening the door to the outside.

The door opened onto the central square of Greymoss Rest. Endymion and Lily stepped out into the morning sun. Most of the village had gathered there. A group of fifteen or so were trying to form a military line near the closed gate.

Endymion half-recognized several people from the day he'd first stumbled into Greymoss Rest. They looked far less formidable now that he wasn't flat on his back beneath them. A few swords and knives glittered menacingly, but most held improvised weapons, like farm implements and rough wooden clubs. He spotted a pitchfork, a woodman's axe, and several sickles.

Another group clustered near Sorrel's door; Sorrel among them. They were having an animated discussion in their high, lilting language. The conversation slowed as several of them turned to look at Endymion and Lily. Endymion assumed they were members of the Rootcircle.

A man broke from the circle, striding toward Endymion and Lily, his shoulders stiff and eyes burning. "You've brought this upon us!" he said. "It's going to be another Red Spring. You've led doom to our door!" Endymion recognized the voice— it was Oran, the one Sorrel had referred to as the Taproot, the center of the circle. His mouth was pinched tight as if he'd bitten into something bitter and never quite recovered.

A woman near the group shifted, eyes narrowing. A murmur rippled through the crowd. Someone tightened their grip on a sickle.

Sorrel stepped up, lifting her hands in a quieting gesture. "Oran," she said. "Calm." Her voice caught slightly on the word. "We don't know that this will go that way."

Oran looked up at Endymion, turned his head to the side, and spat on the ground. "When has his kind ever brought anything but death here?" he said.

There was a tower on the inside of the wall. It looked more like a lookout post than a defense—just tall enough for someone at the top to see what was beyond without being seen. A young man, barely older than Endymion or Lily, came charging down from the tower. He sprinted across the square toward the circle and called out, "The Móra—the one on the big horse—says we're to come out. Now!"

Both sides of the wooden gate creaked partway open at once. The Wee Folk who were pulling the gates grunted and strained. This morning was the first time the doors had ever been shut—or opened. Now, they resisted opening as stubbornly as they'd resisted closing.

The Wee Folk line wavered, then stiffened again, each doing their best to look fierce. It was hard to look uniform when you held a sickle and the person beside you carried a pitchfork.

Outside the gate, the duke's soldiers stood in a crisp, silent line, their brown tabards neat and unrumpled. Their spears formed a metal thicket. The banner-man held the duke's sigil with the black silhouette of the stag. It flapped boldly in the morning breeze.

The captain urged his horse forward, Godric on one side and Ned on the other. He held the rest of his men back with a raised hand.

Oran sighed, shook his head, and muttered, "If they think we'll roll over like sheep, they're wrong."

He glanced at Sorrel and another member of the Circle. "Are we ready?" he said.

As they started toward the gate, Oran threw a look over his shoulder at Endymion and Lily. "Someone bring him," he said, but no one responded. He didn't repeat himself.

Endymion slid the well-shaped but unfamiliar crutches under his arms and followed the three circle members. Lily hurried up to support him. She shot a glance at Oran, then reached up to grip Endymion's forearm. He looked down and met her eyes. For a moment, Endymion thought he understood why Sorrel referred to the connection between them as a soul-thread. He felt the warmth of Lily's heart reaching out to his own.

As the three Wee Folk officials crossed through the gate, Endymion and Lily following behind, Oran spoke to the people manning the doors. "Be ready to close those again," he said. "As quickly as you can if things start to go wrong."

T he Wee Folk delegation approached, the captain and his escorts advancing from the other side until the two groups faced each other in an uneasy set of parallel lines. Endymion and Lily stood just behind the three Circle members; Godric and Ned flanked the captain.

A tense silence followed—no one seemed to know what to say.

The silence was broken when Sorrel said cheerfully, "Good morning! It's a beautiful day. What can we do for you?" Oran shot her a grim sidelong look.

The captain looked momentarily startled, but Sorrel's unexpected tone didn't seem to deter him from his planned opening. "I am here as a representative of Lord Cuthred, Baron of the Western Marches."

Oran looked about to speak, but Sorrel interjected before he could. "And?" she said calmly, as if coaxing a hesitant child to speak in front of a class.

The captain looked over the crowd—tired faces, anxious ones. He'd seen the aftermath of skirmishes before. He didn't want to see another.

"As you know," he continued, "the baron rules these western lands, from Ashton in the north to the realm of the Sword of the South." He hesitated. "Under the rule of our Good King Twilight, of course."

Oran turned his head to one side and spat demonstratively into the dirt. Ned flinched.

The captain went on, unfazed. "King Twilight has charged all the soldiers under his command to guard the kingdom's peace."

The captain's jaw tightened. "A grievance has been

raised." He scanned the Circle leaders—then locked his eyes on Endymion.

Endymion's throat tightened. He didn't like the feeling that this was about him.

There was a moment of silence. The Wee Folk stared up at the soldier, waiting to hear what he was going to say next.

Godric, who had been fidgeting and shifting to and fro beside the captain, suddenly spoke. "That's all you're going to do?" he said, his voice sharp with frustration. "That's it? Register a complaint?"

Lily shifted beside Endymion and brushed his hand—just once, just enough.

The captain looked at Godric sternly and said, "That's my charge. What did you expect me to do? What did you want?"

Godric went still, his fidgeting forgotten, and stared down at the dirt. "I... I don't know."

The captain turned away from Godric, as if from an unpleasant task completed, and addressed the Wee Folk contingent again. "The nature of the grievance is that a young boy—presumably you," he said, nodding at Endymion, "—has been stolen or seduced from Woolfold in the Dell."

He looked more directly now. "Son, are you here of your own free will?"

Endymion shifted his weight. Pain shot through his ankle —but it anchored him. He looked around at the silent crowd, the spears, the sidelong looks. He saw Lily beside him, her fingers twitching, as if holding back from reaching for his hand.

"I don't know much about free will," he said at last, his voice quiet but carrying. "But I know this: no one took me. No one lured me. I followed *her*."

He looked at Lily—fully. Openly.

"She didn't ask. I followed because I wanted to. Because I couldn't imagine not knowing her. Not seeing her. Not walking the same road."

There was a silence. Oran started to step forward, but Sorrel's hand on his arm stopped him. Her eyes said everything: *Not now.*

"I'm not going back," Endymion said. "Not without her. And if we're not welcome there—" He turned, facing Oran now, "—then we'll find another road. Together."

The wind stirred again. A faint breath moved through the trees.

Lily reached for his hand, this time without hesitation. She laced her fingers through his.

"I'm not a prize to be stolen," she said. "And he's not a

sheep to be herded back to the fold."

The captain watched them for a moment, unreadable. Then he nodded once.

"I think we're done here."

Godric stepped forward, face flushing red. "No!" he shouted. "You're letting them go? Just like that? What about the fruit? What about the old laws? You were supposed to stop this! This is how it always begins—with spells and seductions. You've heard the stories!"

The captain looked down at him as one might glance at a barking dog. "King Twilight charged us with keeping peace, not punishing love." He didn't say it like a formality, but like a prayer he believed in. "Take your grievances to the Moot, goodman."

Godric opened his mouth again—then shut it. His eyes flicked toward the watching crowd, the murmurs already starting to rise. No one would come to his defense.

The captain wheeled his horse and trotted back toward his men. Godric stared, slack-jawed, but said nothing more.

A murmur rippled through the watching villagers, as the crowd slowly exhaled the breath they'd been holding.

Sorrel murmured to no one in particular, "Well. That went better than expected."

In the final days of spring that year, before the season eased into summer, a strange thing happened. The fire lily flowers, which, it was known, only bloomed after fire swept across a hillside, blossomed across the hills and valleys between Woolfold in the Dell and Greymoss Rest.

The mountain ridges and slopes turned red. Red as the setting sun. Red as a glowing ember from a campfire where lovers had met for an evening tryst. Red as spilled wine. Red as blood.

Some said that the end of that spring was unseasonably hot, and the heat had coaxed the flowers into blooming early.

Some compared it to the way oak trees all drop their acorns in unison, as if the plants were speaking to one another.

A few thought that maybe Sorrel and her husband—the Herbmother and Greenwarden of the village of Greymoss Rest —might have used some potion or spell to cause the plants to blossom out of turn. Possibly as a gift to their daughter.

But in the end, it doesn't matter.

From that year on, "The Red Spring" meant something different in the little sheep-herding village of Woolfold in the Dell.

D arkness cloaked Marj's shop. A single flickering candle-flame held back the gloom of night. The cunning woman sat at her workbench, watching what might have been an errant moonbeam creeping into the room through an opening near the roof.

The glimmering moonlight illuminated the wall, revealing a set of runes, arranged across the place where the light fell. To a stranger, it might have looked like a sundial—or a moondial, rather.

The beam touched the last rune. Marj gave a grunt. "Midnight." She pulled a soft lambskin cover from the object in front of her. It was a sphere of crystal. The candlelight danced across its partially reflective surface.

Marj passed a hand just above the crystal's cold upper edge. The interior grew cloudy, like breath fogging glass.

She peered into the depths. For a moment, nothing changed. Then the clouds parted, like sunlight breaking through an overcast sky, and a face appeared.

Marj blinked. It was always disconcerting to look down into her crystal and feel, somehow, like she was peering up from the other side.

"Good evening," said Sorrel.

The image of the Wee Folk woman's face rippled. Marj knew she was looking up from a basin in Sorrel's stillroom—an enchanted pool of water. They had discussed the differences between Wee Folk magic and the cunning arts. They had exchanged knowledge slowly, steadily—things no one else, perhaps, had ever known.

Marj nodded in response to Sorrel's greeting. "It's done," she said.

"Aye," said Sorrel. "And done well, I think."

"They can never know," said Marj. She frowned. "Helen, too." She looked away from the crystal, staring at the moonbeam on the wall. "We undid sixteen years of bloody stupidity."

Sorrel looked sympathetically at her friend. "They really love each other, you know." She shook her head. "We only gave fate a push." She hesitated, before adding, "I never lied. I said I couldn't break a soul-thread. I never said we couldn't weave one."

Marj met Sorrel's gaze through the crystal and water, and said almost grudgingly, "I've seen worse matches—born of moonlight, foolish dreams, and charmed into place. These two? They've got something real."

Within the crystal, Sorrel nodded and traced a gesture over the water. Her face—and the light within the crystal—faded together, leaving just the flickering candle and the moon.

Outside, the hills waited quietly beneath the moonlight. Morning would come soon, warm and bright—with it, the soft laughter of two souls who had never meant to be woven together, but now could not be pulled apart.

L ily gave Endymion a skeptical look. "Sometimes I think you're as slow as one of your sheep," she said. Urania bleated mournfully nearby. "Oh, I didn't mean you, Urania," said Lily. "I was referring to one of the other ones." The morning sun cut through the fog. This was the hour Endymion and Lily loved the meadow best.

Urania's head moved as if she were nodding, though it could have been just her reaching down for her next bite of grass. Then she bleated again, this time with what sounded suspiciously like judgment.

Lily continued, "We can't live in Woolfold." She poked Endymion playfully in the ribs. He tried to catch her finger, but she pulled it away. Then her tone shifted. "They still don't like me there."

"I didn't mean for us to live there," said Endymion. "I was thinking of it more as a staging ground. A place where we could prepare for our travels."

"And what would those travels be, exactly?" asked Lily, though they had already discussed this.

"Liamec," said Endymion. "I want to see the bottomless Dragon's Gorge. I want to look out from the ramparts of the King's Seat across the endless towers and battlements. I want to catch a talking fish, like Caspian Fisher of Chelle by the Sea. I want to fight a blue-haired pirate of Meara—and win."

"We," said Lily quietly. "*We* want to do those things."

EPILOGUE

The trail between Greymoss Rest and Woolfold in the Dell was open once more. One of the first to use it—aside from Lily and Endymion—was Marj, heading to visit Sorrel.

Trade slowly resumed between the two villages. The shepherds of Woolfold found the goods from Greymoss Rest—especially the dyes—surprisingly enticing.

Godric lost his long-held position as Voice of the Moot when he refused to accept that the renewed trail and trade with Greymoss Rest were here to stay.

Ellie was patient and kind. Eventually, Leland saw her. She, of course, had always had eyes for him.

Urania, emboldened by her adventures, made the daring step from last sheep in the flock to second from last.

Endymion and Lily left the mountains behind and explored the land of Liamec. They found Capitol—the capital city of Liamec—especially interesting. Endymion had never thought that he might meet a king.

But the road was theirs now, and it stretched on, as wide and full of wonder as the land of Liamec itself.

But those are tales for another time.

Dear Reader,

Thank you for reading *Endymion and the Fae*. I hope you enjoyed your time in the mountain meadows and misty woods of Liamec.

Like many of the *Tales of Liamec*, this story stands on its own— but the world is full of quiet echoes and hidden threads. If you haven't yet read *The Wolf's Tooth* or *By the Sea*, you might enjoy seeing how some themes, places, and legends connect across the series. And if you already have, I hope a few moments here felt like glimpsing something familiar from a new path.

If this story brought you joy, I'd be truly grateful if you left a quick review on Amazon. Your words help others discover these books—and help me keep writing them.

With thanks,
J. Steven Lamperti

ACKNOWLEDGEMENT

Thanks to my beta readers, John, Claudia and Page.

Also, as always, to my alpha, Andrea.

BOOKS IN THIS SERIES

The tales of Liamec

The Wolf's Tooth

"A gripping read that is hard to put down." — The BookLife Prize

Raised by wolves. Bound for destiny. Hunted for a secret he doesn't yet understand.

Twee never chose the wild, but it raised him all the same. From his first toddling steps among wolf pups to nights curled in their den, the forest was his only home.

But the world beyond the trees is harsher—outlaws and city streets, forge smoke and forgotten poor. In Grisput, Twee learns the blacksmith's trade and crosses paths with a red-haired street girl who carries magic in her pockets and secrets she dares not reveal. Whispers of prophecy circle closer, until even the King's Guard begins to listen.

For readers who love A Wizard of Earthsea and Stardust, The Wolf's Tooth begins in whimsy and deepens into wonder —a heartfelt coming-of-age fantasy about kinship found in unexpected places, and strength discovered in the quiet heart of a boy who never asked to be special.

Step into the forest. Follow the smoke. The journey begins where the wild things run.

By The Sea

"An entertaining tale that is all its own." — The BookLife Prize

The sea took her brother. Now it whispers her name.

Years after the storm that claimed his life, Annabelle Fisher still walks the shoreline—but keeps her heart turned away from the sea, and from anyone whose eyes dance with the waves.

When a handsome stranger brings an invitation to the duke's castle, one dance pulls her into a world of ocean-born secrets and ancient rivalries. The castle looms on the cliffs above Chelle by the Sea, yet the fisher-folk rarely climb the winding path to its gates. Annabelle's steps there will carry her farther than she ever imagined.

But the ball is only the beginning. Annabelle's path will lead beneath the earth, into shadowed places where only the gods dare to dwell—and where love may cost her everything.

Though part of the Tales of Liamec, Annabelle's journey can be read alone—like a single tide in a wider sea.

Told with the lilt of folklore and the sweep of myth, By the Sea is a lyrical YA fantasy of loss, courage, and ocean magic—perfect for fans of The Scorpio Races and The Girl Who Drank the Moon.

The tide is rising. Follow Annabelle beyond the breakers.

Twilight's Fall

"…a gripping tale of how a young king fights hard to redeem his throne." — Pearly Chit Chat's About Books

A quiet guardsman. A young king. A peace about to be broken.

Corentin never sought glory. His duty was simple: guard the crown and serve in silence. But when an ambush shatters King Twilight's journey home, Corentin finds himself fleeing with the young monarch—and two unlikely companions: Aela, an herbalist with steady hands, and Blaine, a fellow guard who escaped the slaughter at his side.

What begins in loyalty deepens into friendship, and what starts as flight grows into open war. As betrayal spreads through the realm and the dead begin to stir, Corentin must face a legacy he never asked for—and summon the strength to protect a kingdom on the brink.

Blending myth, quiet heroism, and fierce battles—with a thread of slow-burning romance—Twilight's Fall is a richly woven fantasy for readers who believe friendships can be as fateful as crowns.

Twilight is falling. Loyalty will decide the dawn.

The Channeler Trilogy

"…a fantasy world that draws readers in and keeps them turning the pages." — Reader Review

The entire collected Channeler Trilogy—Moon & Shadow, Sun & Dream, and Death & Dragon—in one sweeping volume.

A moon misplaced. A girl who dreams too well. A world beginning to bend.

Sebastian never asked to be a hero. But when nightmare creatures rise from the shadows, he finds himself gathering strange objects—gifts tied to a quiet girl named Anise, whose dreams stir ancient forces.

As years pass and old stories deepen, Anise steps from the edges of his tale into the heart of her own. At the Academy, she begins to shape the world that once shaped her, forging bonds with forgotten gods and walking the boundary between dreams and waking.

Spanning seasons, generations, and shifting destinies, The Channeler Trilogy is a sweeping, heartfelt tale of magic, friendship, and the courage to claim your place in a changing world.

Perfect for fans of A Wizard of Earthsea and Stardust.

The dream is stirring. Follow it to the end.

Sunshine Over Hero

Strange things are happening in the village of Hero.

First it was the sheep—found drained of blood. Then village girls began to disappear, returning days later with no memory of where they'd been.

Sunny, a sharp-minded farm girl with no patience for nonsense, is sure something unnatural is behind it. But when Raphael shows up—a traveling monster hunter whose last case was a mouse spirit stealing cheese—she realizes help might not be as heroic as she needs.

Raphael does have a few advantages: a talking silver sword named Cutter, a fire imp named Iggy who only ever says "Burn," and a willingness to follow Sunny's lead. The only problem? Cutter's eloquence and Iggy's enthusiasm don't always mix.

As the mystery deepens, the two uncover an ancient threat—and a connection neither expected.

Though part of the Tales of Liamec, Sunshine and Raphael's tale can be read alone—its own romp through fangs and fire.

Sunshine Over Hero is a romantic fantasy full of magic, mischief, and just a touch of bite—perfect for fans of Howl's Moving Castle and Legends & Lattes.

The Pirates Of Meara

A silver-eyed girl washes ashore, and nothing in Mouse's life is quiet again.

Fern is a duke's daughter, stolen by pirates and cast adrift in a city she doesn't understand.
Mouse is a street orphan who thought he knew Meara—until the city begins whispering secrets only he can hear.

Now the pirate Bluebeard hunts them both—but the truth runs deeper, hidden in stone and salt.
Because Mouse isn't just a quiet boy with a borrowed name—he's the key to an undersea world the city has not forgotten.

Though part of the Tales of Liamec, Mouse and Fern's voyage can be read alone—a harbor for new readers.

The Pirates of Meara is a gentle, magical tale of friendship, lost cities, and tides that pull us home—perfect for fans of The Chronicles of Prydain and The True Confessions of Charlotte Doyle.